A MESSAGE F

Dawson handed Kirk [...] colored ribbon.

"Mr. Spock's message[...] brought it to me at the in[...]

As Kirk untied the ribbon and opened the scroll, Scotty watched Dawson remove his garishly marked, close-fitting hood, displaying his newly shaven head.

"What were you doing down there, Lieutenant? Playing trick or treat?"

Dawson grinned and rubbed his head. "My—"

Kirk's voice suddenly halted further conversation. His face a frozen mask, he spoke in unnaturally calm, precise tones.

"Mr. Scott, please call the engine room and have your people check on the status of the trilithium modulator crystals. Also have them check stores to see if the replacements are there."

"Now why would you be wanting the trilithium modules checked out at a time like this?"

"Please carry out my orders, Mr. Scott," Kirk said. Although he gave no hint of inner turmoil, there was a quality to his voice that made Scott jump.

"Aye, aye, sir."

"Jim, what the hell's wrong?" McCoy asked. Kirk ignored him, staring at the scroll in his hands.

Scott went to the communicator and began to snap orders to his duty officers. When they replied, their voices were high and excited. Scott turned to his captain, his broad face ashen.

"They're gone! The replacements, too! Our warp drive is disabled!"

"Then Spock wasn't bluffing," Kirk said in a low voice. "Gentlemen, I regret to inform you that the *Enterprise* and her crew are at the mercy of a madman. Mr. Spock has gone insane."

Bantam Star Trek titles

PERRY'S PLANET
PLANET OF JUDGMENT
SPOCK, MESSIAH!
WORLD WITHOUT END

SPOCK, MESSIAH!

Theodore R. Cogswell
and
Charles A. Spano, Jr.

**(Based on the Television Series
Created by GENE RODDENBERRY)**

BANTAM BOOKS
TORONTO • NEW YORK • LONDON • SYDNEY • AUCKLAND

SPOCK, MESSIAH!

A Bantam Book / September 1976

2nd printing ... October 1976	*4th printing ... February 1978*
3rd printing ...... June 1977	*5th printing ... October 1984*

ISBN 0-553-24674-7

Published simultaneously in the United States and Canada.

Bantam Books are published by Bantam Books, Inc. Its trade-
mark, consisting of the words "Bantam Books" and the por-
trayal of a rooster, is registered in the United States Patent
Office and in other countries. Marca Registrada. Bantam
Books, Inc., 666 Fifth Avenue, New York, New York 10103.

PRINTED IN THE UNITED STATES OF AMERICA

H   14 13 12 11 10 9 8 7 6 5

SPOCK, MESSIAH!

CHAPTER ONE

Captain's log. Stardate 6720.8.

This is our eighth day in orbit around the Class M planet, Kyros. Dr. McCoy has reported that initial trials of the telescan cephalic implants devised by Starfleet Cultural Survey Bureau have been generally successful. Though some survey team members complained of disorientation on first being linked with the Kyrosian minds, Dr. McCoy is confident that once each team member realizes he can consciously control the feelings of personality intrusion caused by the link, present complaints of feeling like two different people simultaneously will cease.

Successful completion of our mission on Kyros will mean the acceptance of the telescan implant as a routine survey tool.

Captain James T. Kirk, commanding the United Starship *Enterprise*, pressed his forefinger against a button on the log computer's control panel, shutting it off.

He yawned and stretched. The survey team had been beamed down for its third day on Kyros early that morning while he was still asleep. His watch had been strictly routine and a bit boring. He was looking forward to a long drink, a good meal, and an hour or so of solitude before the debriefing later that evening when the survey team was beamed up for the night.

He leaned back in his thickly padded black command chair and gazed around the bridge of the great starship, nodding his approval of the quiet efficiency with which the bridge crew went about the complex and demanding business of running the *Enterprise*.

The bridge was a circular chamber located on the

top deck of the huge, saucer-shaped, detachable primary hull. It began to his left with the main engineering console, currently manned by Lt. Comdr. Montgomery Scott, and continued around to the ship's environmental control console, engineering sub-systems monitor station, the visual display monitor—a viewing screen which could show any part of the ship's exterior, but which now showed cloud-wreathed Kyros turning in its orbit some sixteen hundred kilometers below—then on to the defense sub-systems monitor, defense and weapons console, navigation, main computer and science station, now manned by the second science officer, Lt. Comdr. Helman, and lastly communications, where Lt. Uhura, a lovely woman of Bantu descent, was setting up another scanning program for the normal light and infra-red cameras trained on Kyros.

Directly in front of Kirk was a double console containing the navigator's station on the right and the helmsman's on the left.

Kirk raised his brown eyes from the twin console and studied the view of Kyros on the visual monitor. As he watched the televised image, he heard the turbo-lift's doors hiss open behind him.

Navigator Vitali and Helmsman Shaffer swiveled in their seats and nodded to the entering officers.

Kirk turned and waved a greeting at the approaching pair.

"Lieutenant Sulu . . ." began one.

"Ensign Chekov . . ." chimed in the other.

". . . reporting for duty, sir," they finished simultaneously.

Kirk smiled. "Carry on, gentlemen, and a good evening to you both."

The two officers—Lt. Sulu, an Oriental of mixed ancestry but with Japanese predominating, born on Alpha Mensa Five; and Ensign Pavel Chekov, a terrestrial Russian with bushy black hair and a round, youthful face—took their seats at the combined console in front of the captain, as their off-duty counterparts stood and stretched luxuriously.

"A long watch, Ensign Shaffer?" Kirk asked the young man.

Shaffer nodded and said, "Aye, sir." He gestured toward the image of Kyros on the monitor screen.

"The first few days aren't too bad; a new planet's always sort of interesting, but after a while it can be a drag." The ensign quickly added, ". . . sir."

"After the long run out here, just sitting with nothing to do is pleasant," the female navigator said. "Some of the courses I had to plot were a little hairy. Opening up star routes in an uncharted sector of the galaxy can put wrinkles on a girl."

"We were lucky, Lieutenant," Kirk said. "Finding life in only the third system we visited was like throwing ten sevens in a row."

"Well," said Sulu, "a routine one-on and two-off schedule with no problems for three hundred parsecs is infinitely preferable to spending the rest of your life as, for instance, the plaything of a superpowerful alien juvenile delinquent."*

"Small chance of that happening here, Mr. Sulu," Kirk said with a chuckle. "The Kyrosians have a D+ rating on the Richter Cultural Scale, at least the city-dwelling lowlanders do. The hill clans are fairly primitive nomadic herdsmen, as far as we have determined. When Spock and the rest of the survey party beam up tonight, we should be able to fill in the blanks. But you can relax, Sulu; we've picked up enough to know that there's nothing down there that's a threat to the *Enterprise.*"

"In that case, sir," Shaffer said, "Lieutenant Vitali and I are going to devote the first part of the evening to the pursuit of a thick pair of Terran beefsteaks." Turning to the woman, he asked, "Care to chart a course in that direction, Navigator?"

As the pair stepped up a short flight of stairs to the upper part of the deck and entered the turbo-lift, Kirk gave the bridge a last quick glance.

---

*See: *"The Squire of Gothos,"* STAR TREK 2, Bantam Books, 1968.

"Everything seems to be in order," Kirk said. "Mr. Sulu, you'll take the con this watch." He glanced to his left and saw Engineering Officer Scott stretching. "Ready to call it a day, Scotty?"

The big, bluff, red-haired Scotsman nodded and his relief, Lt. Leslie, slipped into the padded black swivel seat at the console.

"But, Captain," Scott began in a thick burr, which somehow disappeared completely when he was under stress, "d'ye think it's a gude idea to leave the *Enterprise* in the hands of sic a wee lad as Sulu?" He flicked his left eyelid at Kirk.

Kirk caught the wink, and fell in with the jovial feud between Scott and Sulu, which had been underway ever since a debate over the merits of hot saki, as opposed to Scotch.

"As helm officer," Scott added lugubriously, "the bairn may be able to hold orbit—gie'en the proper supervision o'course—but the con, now; I think it's a bit more o' a load than those young shoulders can bear."

Kirk gave a mock frown. "You've a good point there, Scotty."

Sulu swung partway around in his seat to gaze in astonishment at the muscular captain who stood staring at him, hands on hips.

"But, if Chekov could just keep an eye on things . . ." Kirk went on. "How about it, Navigator? If Sulu should start pushing the wrong buttons and send the *Enterprise* out of orbit and into a nose dive, do you think you could show him how to get back?"

Chekov glanced at Sulu, then looked away. Helman snickered.

"I'll do my best, Captain," he said in a Russian accent so thick the last word sounded like "kyptin." "But would you straighten me out one more time . . . Do I push the green button for Up or the red one?"

"Don't tell him, sir," Scott said. "Let him find out the hard way."

Laughing, the two officers turned and mounted the stairs to the raised deck, the engineering officer slightly ahead. As they were about to enter the turbo-lift, Chekov leaned forward, studying the screens on his console intently.

"Captain!"

Kirk swung around. "What is it, Mr. Chekov?"

"The scanners have picked up a radiation front coming toward us on course . . ." Chekov paused, did some fine tuning, then continued, ". . . on course 114, mark 31."

"Intensity reading?" Kirk asked levelly.

"Intensity two at the moment, but a narrow scan indicates the beginning of a build-up."

Kirk stepped briskly to the science console on the raised deck. "Mr. Helman, verify please," he ordered, now all starship commander rather than bantering superior. As Helman bent over his instruments, Scott moved back to the engineering console and began to perform his own operations.

Moments later, Helman straightened up and said, "Something's coming in, all right. How do you read, Mr. Scott?"

"I can verify Chekov's readings, too, but there's nae to worrie aboot. The hull shielding's good to intensity twenty. If the front builds beyond that, we can put up the deflector screens. Except for a nova's blast, they'll stop anything long enou' for us to leave the vicinity."

"Mr. Helman, if you please," Kirk said as he stepped to the science console. His strong fingers moved over the colored controls pressing and switching. He studied the results displayed in a small viewing screen.

"I thought so . . . Mr. Helman, do you see it?" Kirk asked the science officer. "I thought it looked a little odd." Helman murmured agreement. Turning, Kirk said, "Mr. Sulu, tie the science scanners in with the navigation computer. I want a time factor on that."

"Aye, sir," the officer responded and turned with brisk attention to his console.

Kirk remained standing at the science station, but he could see Sulu's slim fingers dance across the double board. Scott followed suit, running a parallel check.

Sulu suddenly let out a low whistle.

"Problem?" Kirk asked.

"Could be, sir. I'll recheck," Sulu replied.

"Ye don't have to," Scott said. "My readout checks with yours." His thick, blunt fingers pressed several switches and a spectrographic image of Kyros' sun appeared on the forward visual monitor blanking out the image of the planet.

Kirk looked at the picture and heard Scott mutter, "That dinna make sense."

"Explain," Kirk ordered. He glanced back at the screen as Scott began to talk.

"That radiation front shows a Doppler shift to the violet; a primary sign o' a star gaein' nova. But yon spectrograph shows Kyr as quiet an' calm as a sleepin' babe. It's still a placid G5."

"Are there any novae or supernovae in this quadrant?" Kirk asked Helman.

The science officer replied, frowning, "None detectable, sir. The only possible candidate is a blue Class B main sequence star about nine parsecs away, out of range of our longest range scanners. However, assuming it did blow thirty years ago, the front just reaching us now wouldn't be much beyond point oh-oh-one because of the square of the distance and all."

"It has me worried, too, Commander," Kirk said, noting the frown. "If we don't know where it is, we can't be sure of which direction to run in order to avoid it."

"To run, sir?" Uhura asked from the communications console.

"It's a possibility right now, Lieutenant," Kirk said. He turned back to study the peaceful spectrograph still on the monitor. "All right, gentlemen, keep after it. I want to know as much about that front as we can learn in the shortest possible time. If you haven't licked it by the time Spock and the others beam up, I'll detail him to help you." Kirk's voice took on a small note of worry. "If he's feeling up to it."

Uhura spoke up again, concern in her voice. "What's wrong with Mr. Spock?" Her deep respect for both the captain and the half-human first officer sometimes manifested itself in a maternal fashion.

"He's been feeling the effects of his implant a little more strongly than the others on the survey detail, though he's assured me he can control it," Kirk replied. "If he's still acting as strangely as he did the night before last, I'll have to order McCoy to remove it. It seems that Mr. Spock's dop is giving him a real migraine."

"Dop?" Scott asked as he walked from the engineering console to the gap in the rail which ran around the inner edge of the upper deck. "What the divil is a dop?"

"Dop is from an old German word—*doppleganger* —meaning the ghostly double of a living person. Ensign George made it up," Kirk replied.

He peered at the monitor screen a final time. "I'll be in my quarters until the team is beamed up. Keep on that front and call me if there's any change." He turned to Scott. "Coming, Mr. Scott?"

Once in his cabin, Kirk lay down on his bunk. Behind him, and built into the bulkhead, was a cabinet. Kirk reached back, rolling over onto his stomach as he did so. From a small shelf of real books, rather than microtapes, he took a dog-eared copy of Xenophon's *Anabasis*. He flopped onto his back, opened the book, and began to read for the hundredth time that ancient Greek's account of being trapped in hostile territory a thousand miles from home, and of the months of battles, marches, and countermarches until, at long last, the small army of mercenaries arrived safely home. Unstated in the matter-of-fact account, but apparent behind the scenes, was the loneliness of command, the agonizing decisions that time and again had saved the isolated band from certain destruction. Kirk approved of Xenophon. Born a few millennia later, that worthy would have made a brilliant starship commander.

The captain had just reached the point in the battle of Cunaxa where the Persian commander Cyrus was killed, when the intraship communicator bleeped.

"Kirk here."

"Transporter Room One, Lieutenant Rogers, sir. Lieutenant Dawson requests permission to have Ensign George and Lieutenant Peters beamed up ahead of schedule. He says they're both having dop trouble."

"What kind?"

"The beggar Peters is linked with also picks pockets. Peters says that if he gets preoccupied and forgets to override his dop's normal behavioral patterns, his hands keep sliding into other people's pockets. He finds it so distracting that he can't concentrate on his duties."

"And Ensign George?"

"She can't seem to keep her hands off men, sir—and vice versa."

Kirk sighed. Every time he decided to allow himself the luxury of spending a few hours with his nose in a book, something came along to spoil it.

"Permission granted. Beam them up and tell them to report to Dr. McCoy. Are the rest of the party having any similar problems?"

"Nothing they can't handle, sir."

"How about Commander Spock?"

"I don't know, sir. He hasn't reported in since he beamed down yesterday morning. That's not like him."

"He's probably on the trail of something 'fascinating,'" Kirk said. "We'll hear all about it when he beams up tonight. Kirk out."

He cut communication, looked longingly at his book, closed it reluctantly, and put it to one side. He switched on the intraship communicator again and called the sickbay.

The voice that answered belonged to the ship's chief medical officer, Dr. Leonard McCoy, the only member of the crew with whom the captain could associate on terms of human friendship rather than command.

"Evening, Bones. We've got problems," Kirk began.

"Anything serious?" McCoy asked.

"The dop links," Kirk continued. "Drawing on a native's brain for language and other behavior is great in theory, especially when the native isn't aware of it. But too much is coming across in some cases. Two of

Dawson's party are having trouble controlling the dop input and he's asked to have them beamed up early. I've given permission and told them to report to you, but I'd rather you put someone else on it and come up to my quarters. I'd like to discuss this whole thing."

"Sure thing, Jim," McCoy replied amiably. "I'll have Mbenga handle it, he helped with the original surgery. I'll also bring along a little something to help lubricate our thinking."

It was going to be a long evening. Kirk stripped, stepped into a shower cabinet set in one bulkhead, and set it for frigid needle spray. He gasped as the high pressure jets buffeted his taut, muscular body, massaging and cleansing at the same time. The water cut off abruptly and was replaced by a blast of hot air which dried him in seconds. He stepped out of the cabinet and pulled on a fresh uniform.

"Good timing, Bones," he said as his cabin door hissed open and McCoy stepped in. The doctor carried a peculiarly shaped flask of an amber-colored drink, Canopian brandy, Kirk's favorite.

He set the curved flask down on Kirk's desk, took two snifter glasses from the wainscot cabinet which ran along the inner bulkhead, and filled each glass halfway. He handed one to Kirk, and the two stood silently for a moment, sipping the potent brandy slowly and appreciatively.

McCoy's seamed, leathery face peered at Kirk over the rim of the glass he held, his dark blue eyes fixed on his captain, waiting for him to speak.

"Ahhh, lovely! Much better than that green Saurian stuff you like, eh, Bones?" Kirk said. He held out his glass. "A little more."

"I'm an equal opportunity drinker, Jim," McCoy remarked. "Here you are." The doctor refilled Kirk's glass, then his own.

The two men sat and began to discuss the malfunctioning of the telescan implants. McCoy frowned as Kirk described the reasons for the early return of two of the survey team members.

McCoy let out a sudden, startled whistle when Kirk relayed Dawson's report on Ensign George's problem.

"Sara did that?" he said incredulously. "Jim, she couldn't have. She's the starchiest female I've run into in years. I gave her a friendly pat one day and she almost took my head off. It's a shame such a lovely woman should have such anachronistic beliefs about the human body." McCoy shook his head, then asked Kirk, "Have you had much of a chance to talk with her?"

Kirk shook his head.

"She's on special assignment from Cultural Survey to evaluate the effectiveness of the cephalic implants as a survey tool," McCoy began. "One of her jobs has been selecting likely native matches for survey team linkages. It looks as if she didn't do such a good job on her own. Come to think of it, she was giving Spock the eye when they were getting ready to beam down the day before yesterday."

"Oh, no," groaned Kirk. "Not another one! Why does nearly every woman assigned to the *Enterprise* set her cap for that walking computer? Doesn't she understand Vulcans?"

"I imagine so. She must be aware that Vulcans only have the mating urge—the pon farr—every seven years." McCoy shrugged. "But be that as it may, we're going to have to tune Sara's implant to a new dop. She doesn't seem to be able to handle the one she's linked to now. With all the profiles she had to choose from, I'm surprised she didn't pick one whose personality was more like her own."

"How many Kyrosian profiles do we have?" Kirk asked.

"Over two hundred. Sara did the collecting herself. We picked up enough information by tight-beam scan to be able to outfit her in native dress. She was transported down just outside the city gates at night with a personality scanner hidden in a pouch. When the gates opened in the morning, she pretended to be a mute. Through sign language, she found an inn at the center of town, rented the rooms we're using as a transporter terminal, locked the door, set up the scanner, and began recording natives."

McCoy paused a moment and sipped from his glass. "She beamed up with quite a collection—town people, hill people, even a couple of Beshwa."

"Beshwa?"

"Kyrosian gypsies. Anyway," McCoy continued, "the native neural patterns she recorded on mag-cards give detailed personality profiles as distinctive as fingerprints.

"The next step was to select the profile that would be most useful to a particular survey party member in his particular mission, tune a telescan implant to it, and insert it surgically behind his right ear. Once it was turned on, a telepathic link was established with the selected native that gives the investigator an immediate command of idiomatic Kyrosian and the ability to react behaviorally in any situation exactly as his dop would."

Kirk gave a wry grin. "And that, as George and Peters found out, can create problems."

"But don't worry, Jim, we'll get the bugs worked out. Even with the minor problems we've encountered so far, the implant is the best survey device the bureau has come up with yet. We picked up more information, so Dobshansky tells me, on how Kyrosian society works in the last few days, than we could have in a month using the old system. Of course we're lucky that the natives are humanoid enough that, except for colored contact lenses that duplicate their unusual eye pigmentation, little is needed in the way of disguise. The links make it possible for our people to go almost anyplace with complete acceptance. Within limits," McCoy added, waving his glass for emphasis. "If you're linked to a street beggar, you're going to behave and talk like one. And that means you won't be able to pass yourself off as a Kyrosian aristocrat. But as I said, we've been rather successful in matching profile to mission, though I should have checked on Ensign George more closely. I'll get her on the operating table tonight and tune her implant to one which isn't so . . . so friendly. I'll see if I can dig up a man-hater so she'll stop pestering Spock."

"I've a better idea," Kirk said. "Why don't we pull her off the survey detail and put her to work with you on the whole problem? And by the way: I'd like to see the circuit diagrams for the implant. I think I'd better find out what makes that thing tick."

"I've programmed them into the computer already, so I can show you right now," McCoy said, sliding from his perch on the desk. He turned around and pulled a vision screen erect from the surface of the desk and pressed the intraship communicator button.

"Computer . . ."

"Recording," replied the flat, feminine voice of the starship's main computer.

"Display the circuitry of the telescan implant on the captain's visual monitor."

"Working," the computer replied, and a moment later a glowing hologram appeared on the vision screen. The diagram was color-coded. Kirk saw what appeared to be thousands of dots strung on layered spiders' webs. The three-level display turned as McCoy made an adjustment.

"Here it is," the doctor said. "The first section, once tuned to a profile of a native, establishes the telepathic link. This second section acts as a feedback shunt to keep the dop from being aware that his brain has been tapped." McCoy traced a path with his finger. "Next is an input filter stage which passes behavioral information but cuts out thoughts of the moment. Having the constant mental chatter that goes on inside everyone's head coming across would be too distracting."

"I know," said Kirk, nodding sober agreement. "That's one of the reasons Spock, like others with telepathic ability, rarely uses his talent. He finds mind-melding an extremely distasteful process."

"Hah!" McCoy snorted. "The real reason is that he doesn't want his pristine computer banks contaminated with a lot of emotionally tainted and questionable data."

"I think you may be right." Kirk laughed. "But, Bones, you know how infernally curious Spock is. I couldn't keep him from this survey with tractor beams!"

McCoy snorted again and turned back to the diagram. "As I was saying, the implant is a honey of a job of psychoelectronic engineering, especially when you consider that all of its circuitry is encapsulated in a half-centimeter sphere."

"This is where the problems must be," McCoy continued, stabbing a forefinger at the input filter stage. "It looks as if this section isn't working as well as the lab tests predicted. Too much of their dops' personalities are leaking into Sara's and Ensign Peters' brains.

"I think I have an idea." McCoy peered at the diagram with pursed lips. "If you do take Ensign George off the detail, she can help me get to work on it at once. Microminiaturized circuitry is tricky to work on, but with a little technical assistance from the engineering department, we shouldn't really have too much trouble ironing out the problem."

"Good," Kirk said approvingly. He held out his empty glass for another refill, then thought better of it. "Guess I'd better hold off," he murmured regretfully. "They'll be beaming up the rest of the survey team soon and I'll have to be at the debriefing. I'm curious as to what Spock has been up to for the last couple of days."

"Me, too," McCoy agreed and looked into his glass. "Maybe I'd better cut off also, if I'm going to be doing surgery tonight."

Kirk pushed the visual monitor back into his desk as McCoy rinsed the glasses in the cubicle provided in the bathroom. He replaced them in the wainscot cabinet and turned to Kirk.

"Come to think of it, if you've got no objection, I'd like to remove Spock's implant as soon as he gets back. He's not essential down there, and I didn't like the idea of implanting him in the first place. Kyrosian emotional makeup is pretty much like ours, and even if Spock was linked to a cold fish, he has enough trouble keeping his human side under control without having things complicated by leakage from his dop."

"Sounds good," Kirk said. "I'd want him to get to work on the source of that radiation front, anyway. The only reason I let him go down was that he insisted so strongly. Sometimes I think his only purpose in life is to keep feeding a new supply of esoteric data into that logical brain. But he did behave oddly . . ."

"I've always thought Spock was odd," McCoy muttered.

". . . after he was transported up last night," Kirk went on, not hearing McCoy's remark. "He had nothing to say at the debriefing and took off by himself when it was over. I've had reports that he spent most of the night wandering around the ship by himself."

Kirk faced the doctor. "Bones, could anything have gone wrong during his operation?"

McCoy considered for a moment. "I doubt it," he replied. "It was a routine insertion; he was the last one done, anyway. When he was linked, I ran a language test. Without having to think about it, he replied in flawless, idiomatic Kyrosian. There was the expected period of disorientation because of such intimate contact with an alien personality, but Spock seemed in control of the situation. If I'd thought the linkage would have caused him harm, I'd never have let him beam down.

"But," McCoy went on, "I must admit to feeling a little uneasy about the whole thing, in spite of all the information we've acquired. The bright boys at Starfleet are always cooking up gadgets that violate a person's physical integrity. Having my atoms scrambled every time I go through that damn transporter is bad enough, but hooking one man's nervous system to another's with electronic widgets . . ." He grimaced his distaste. "Be only a matter of time before we're all literally worshipping a transistor, or some bloody thing . . ."

Kirk slapped his medical officer on the shoulder. "Bones, transistors were old stuff two hundred years ago."

"You know what I mean," McCoy grumbled.

"Can't fight progress. If man hadn't kept trying to find ways to do things better, we'd never have climbed down from the trees. We'd still be in them, scratching for fleas and swinging from limb to limb."

"So, now we're swinging from star to star," McCoy said sardonically. "And still scratching. We're as much the slaves of our glands as our ancestors were, and most of our behavior makes as much sense. I hope poor Spock hasn't caught the itch. In spite of his dop's low EQ, I'm concerned about permanent effects on that finely tuned Vulcan brain of his."

"Stop fretting," Kirk said. "Spock's used to that sort of thing. It's been a struggle at times, but he's always managed to keep what he considers his illogical side under tight control. Being exposed to a little added irrationality may make him uncomfortable, but Spock's too smart to let it run riot."

The captain grinned slyly at his medical officer.

"You are fond of our Vulcan iceberg, aren't you, Bones?"

McCoy stared at Kirk, harrumphed crustily, and got to his feet.

"I'd better get down to surgery and set up for the removal of Ensign George's implant," he said, unwilling to continue a conversation which might force him to reveal his true feelings for the half-alien first officer. "I'll try to be at the debriefing."

"Hey, Bones," Kirk called.

"Yes?"

"You forgot your bottle."

"Tell you what," McCoy replied. "Keep it. Tomorrow night, put Spock on second watch and we'll lock the door, cut off the communicator, and kill the rest of the bottle. Call it doctor's orders."

Kirk grinned and McCoy stepped toward the cabin's door. He turned suddenly, raising an admonitory finger. "But don't go nipping. That jug punched a nice hole in my budget." McCoy lowered his finger, grinned, and stepped into the corridor.

As the door hissed shut, Kirk lay back down and

picked up his Xenophon. With luck, he could get in a couple of chapters before the survey party came aboard. He had just found his place when the communicator bleeped again.

Kirk dropped the book onto the bunk and went to his desk.

"Kirk here. What is it?" he said, trying to keep annoyance out of his voice.

"Lieutenant Commander Helman, sir," came a worried voice. "We are in condition yellow . . ."

"Specify!" Kirk snapped.

"The radiation front is building. The science computer has projected a geometrical progression on the intensity scale. There's a point 72 probability that the front will pass intensity twenty in the next few days."

Kirk swore silently to himself. That would mean putting up the deflector screens, which would make it impossible to operate the transporters. "Do you have a duration estimate?"

"It's still too early for an accurate prediction, sir," Helman went on. "The computer says that it could die down in a week or two, or go on more than a month. Its configuration is unlike anything in the data banks."

Kirk sighed. "Very good, Commander, thank you. I'll be right up."

He glanced at his book. Scooping both it and his dirty uniform up, he put the book away and tossed the uniform into the autowash chute.

He strode to the door of his quarters wondering when he would finish Xenophon. Then he exited and walked quickly down the corridor to the turbo-lift.

pocketing his Kanopilon. With luck, he could get in a some situation before the next shift pushed away.

CHAPTER TWO

As the turbo-lift doors hissed open, Kirk stepped onto the bridge. Sulu, vacating the command chair, re-seated himself at his helmsman's position.

"Report," Kirk ordered as he sat.

Helman, a tall, thin officer with close-cropped blond hair and a protuberant Adam's apple, straightened from the science console and turned toward the star-ship's captain.

"The radiation front has jumped to intensity 2.4 in the last hour, sir. At first the increase looked like a random fluctuation; but when the computer had enough data to run a curve, it reported a possible condition red, which is when I recommended a yellow alert to Mr. Sulu." Helman gestured at the science console upon which glowed several red lights. "The front has all the char-acteristics of a nova, but the local sun is still perfectly normal."

Captain Kirk frowned. "You can't have a radiation front without a source. Have you backtracked along its course?"

"Aye, sir," Helman replied. "The only star the co-ordinates fit is Epsilon Ionis, the black-hole binary we checked out last month. But how a nova shell could increase in intensity so rapidly . . . It's got me stumped, Captain, and there isn't enough applicable data in the computer to come up with a working hypothesis."

"You will continue to try to pin down that source, but right now I'm more concerned about the possible danger to this ship. We've got to get a more precise reading on the projected radiation increase.

"Lieutenant Leslie," Kirk said, swinging his chair around to face the stocky engineer.

"Sir?"

17

"You and Mr. Sulu will tie in your banks with the science console. I want exact data on the nature of that front."

A chorus of "aye, ayes" sounded, and the officers turned to their consoles to feed in requests, collate incoming data, and to co-ordinate the operations of their stations.

"Ready, sir," Helman said finally.

"Project," Kirk ordered.

The image of Kyros disappeared from the great screen and was replaced by a grid on which each radiational component of the strange shell of energy was plotted on the ordinate against the abscissa of time.

Helman touched a button and, like glowing worms, the component projection lines began to creep across the screen, crawling forward through time and upward in intensity.

"What a hash," Sulu muttered. "It's almost as if we're running into a solar prominence."

Kirk watched intently as the ship's computers continued the projection.

"That readout is getting too complicated," he said. "Blank everything but the hard radiation and high-energy particles, and give me a horizontal on hull shielding safety limits."

The second science officer made a few adjustments and the confusion of the screen began to clear as, one by one, the lines representing the lower frequencies and slower moving particles began to disappear leaving only those charting lethal radiation, high energy protons, alpha particles, and heavy nuclei.

The narrow red line marking the maximum limits of the shields' tolerance flashed on the screen. There was a dead silence on the bridge as the projection track of each component continued an unbroken climb toward the red line.

Suddenly, each of the lines bent sharply and shot upward vertically, slashing the red line in dozens of places and continuing almost to the very top of the grid before peaking and beginning an equally sharp decline.

The ship computer chimed softly and the emotionless

voice began to speak to the silent crew. "Deflector shield activation necessary in eight days, thirteen hours, and twenty-four minutes or radiation penetration will exceed 100 rad."

"And that's enough to put half the crew down with radiation sickness," Kirk muttered.

"At the rate those curves peak," Helman said, nodding agreement with Kirk. "A few more hours' exposure would kill us all, right?"

"Is a response required?" the computer asked.

"We aren't going to be here long enough to make the answer more than academic," Kirk said. "But as long as you have one, let's hear it."

"Data indicates that, unless corrective measures are taken, all crew members, with one exception, will receive a lethal dosage by twenty-three hundred hours, stardate 6728.5."

"Who might be the exception?" Kirk asked. "As if I couldn't guess."

"Commander Spock," said the computer. "Vulcans are twice as resistant to radiation as humans. If an exact prediction of Commander Spock's resistance is desired, a tissue sample must be secured for molecular analyzation."

"That figures," said a familiar voice sardonically. "While the rest of us are heaving and watching our hair fall out, Spock and the computer will be playing three-dimensional chess."

Kirk swung his chair about.

"Bones," he asked, "what are you doing up here? I thought you had our sexpot in surgery."

Dr. McCoy laughed. "I had her on the table, just ready to give her a local when the yellow alert came through. I thought I'd better report to the bridge to see if I was needed, so I told her to report back in the morning. I imagine she's hanging around the transporter room on the odd chance she might get lucky when Spock is beamed up."

He paused and gestured at the visual monitor dominating the front of the bridge.

"Looks like some nasty stuff is on the way in."

" 'Nasty' is an understatement," the captain said. He gazed at the screen thoughtfully for a moment. "In order to weather what will be coming in a few days from now, we'd have to put the shields up, and at the rate that storm is peaking, we'd have to put them on maximum before too long. Twenty hours of that, and the power reserves would be exhausted. If we didn't pull out before then, we'd fry. Buying a few more hours would be pointless anyway. The transporters won't operate while the shields are up, and we've already gathered all the data on Kyros that can be obtained from orbit. There's nothing urgent about the survey, it's mainly a field test for the implants."

Kirk swung his command chair to his right. "Lieutenant Uhura, we're getting out of here. Open a channel to Starfleet, give them our situation, and tell them we're leaving Kyros until things quiet down."

"Aye, sir," Uhura replied. She placed a hypertronic earphone in one ear and turned toward her console.

"In the meantime," Kirk was saying to McCoy, "Spock and his department can pin down the reason for that intensity increase . . ."

Suddenly, he was interrupted by an exclamation from the communications officer.

"Captain, I've lost contact with Starfleet," Uhura said. "I sent out the standard signal, but when I listened for their recognition call, a blast of QRM nearly blew out my eardrum."

"Malfunction, Lieutenant?" Kirk asked.

"Checking now, sir," she replied. Hesitantly, she replaced the earphone and bent over her panel. After a full five minutes of rapid checking, she straightened. "Negative, sir. Everything is in order, but there is something interfering on the sub-space bands."

"That's impossible," Kirk said. "Helman, scan subspace."

The tall science officer bent over his console and moments later snapped upright with a look of surprise. "Computer!" he snapped, "check antenna and sensor circuits for malfunction." He swung toward Kirk who had come out of his chair at Helman's order to the computer. "Captain, you won't believe this . . ."

"All sub-space sensors fully operational," the computer said after a small pause.

"Put it on the main screen," Kirk ordered.

As Helman complied, it was Kirk's turn to feel surprise. The main screen showed a cloud-like formation, vast, pulsing, and ominous. It seemed to swell visibly toward Kirk, expanding outward evenly in all directions. Throughout it, hot spots and radiation peak points flared with rapidity and in close proximity to one another; it seemed as if the bridge crew was peering into the heart of an exploding sun.

"What is that?" Kirk asked.

Helman, looking puzzled, tried to answer. "It's radiation, sir, and it must be a sub-space aspect of the front we've been tracking, but what it's doing down there is beyond me."

"Captain," Chekov said, "it's moving toward us at Warp Ten!"

Kirk stared at Chekov for a moment. "Warp Ten?" He glanced back at the visual monitor. "Whatever it is, Mr. Helman, it's beyond me, too." Looking at Chekov, Kirk said, "Prepare a course, Ensign, 246, Mark 347. Mr. Sulu, we'll move out at Warp Factor Six as soon as the survey party is aboard. Uhura, once we're out of this hash, contact Starfleet, give them a position report, and transmit full information on this radiation."

As the navigator and the helmsman began laying in the course necessary to take the *Enterprise* out of harm's way, Kirk stabbed a button on the arm of the command chair.

"Transporter room," someone replied.

"This is the captain. Has the survey party been beamed up yet?"

"No sir," the transporter officer replied. "They're waiting for Commander Spock. Lieutenant Dawson just checked in and said he's had no word from Mr. Spock all day. I was about to call you, sir."

Kirk frowned at the news. Such behavior was completely uncharacteristic for the precise, punctual science officer. Kirk immediately was afraid something had happened to his Vulcan friend.

"Activate his tingler circuit. Send him the emergency recall signal," Kirk ordered. "I'll keep the communicator open. Let me know as soon as he acknowledges."

"Tingler circuit?" Uhura asked curiously. "What's that?"

"Another idea of the Cultural Bureau," Kirk replied. "An audible signal on the communicators might create a problem in a crowded place, so they came up with a tiny implant that's hooked into a branch of the wearer's sciatic nerve. When activated, it causes a tingling sensation. The wearer then finds a private place and answers the call. If that would take time, the communicator also includes a new circuit. By pushing a button, the wearer can at least acknowledge receiving the signal. But so far Spock has done neither," Kirk finished on a worried note.

"Gadgets in the head, gadgets in the body," grumbled Dr. McCoy. "By the time Survey gets through tucking gadgets inside of us, we'll all be walking machines. I think . . ."

The surgeon was interrupted by the urgent voice of the transporter officer.

"Rogers, again, sir," the officer said. "There's been no reply from Mr. Spock."

Kirk glanced at McCoy. The doctor's eyes were wide. "Home in on his communicator, Lieutenant," Kirk ordered tightly. "Then notify Dawson of the co-ordinates. I want him to get his party to wherever Spock is on the double."

Kirk punched another button, not even acknowledging Rogers' "Aye, sir."

"Security, Kirk here."

"Commander Pulaski, sir," replied the security officer.

"Get a security team to exosociology. Have them outfitted in Kyrosian clothing and issue phasers. Double-check to be sure they're set on low-intensity stun. We may have to beam down for a rescue operation, and I want a minimum amount of force."

"Aye, aye, Captain," Pulaski replied, switching off.

"Do you think that will be necessary, Jim?" McCoy asked.

"I hope not, Bones, I hope not," Kirk replied.

Kirk forced himself to relax as he waited for word of his science officer. McCoy placed a reassuring hand on his shoulder.

"Don't worry, Jim. Old Spock's indestructible. He's never walked into a situation he couldn't handle."

"Captain!" It was the transporter room again.

"Yes?"

"I have Lieutenant Dawson on, but I think you'd better speak to him directly. Mr. Spock wasn't where he was supposed to be."

"Put him on the main visual monitor, Lieutenant," Kirk said. He turned to Uhura. "Pick up Dawson's transmission and patch into the visual on his tricorder."

The communications officer nodded. Pressing several buttons, she picked the transmission up from Kyros. The graph of the radiation storm that was bearing down on the *Enterprise* with increasing intensity disappeared from the screen. There was a flicker and a picture of the inn room below (that served as a rendezvous point and transporter pick-up location for the survey party) appeared. In the center of the picture was a weirdly masked figure. Underneath the mask, Kirk knew, was a young dark-haired lieutenant. He was dressed as a hillman of Kyros.

The most arresting aspect of his costume of leather vest and short cape was the hood, which fitted over the wearer's shaven head. Dawson's was dark blue-dyed leather with white, slanting lines under narrow eye slits. Only his lips were exposed between similar slits. Two small holes let air into his nostrils. A thicker leather cap was sewn onto the hood and slotted, triangular flaps extended below Dawson's nape. Small strings dangled where the hood was laced together along the temples.

"Report," snapped Kirk.

"I must have been given the wrong co-ordinates, sir," Dawson began. "On our grid map of the city, according to the bearings I was given, Mr. Spock, or at least his communicator, was in a small square not far from here. We went there, but it was completely deserted. I took a chance and called the transporter room to check the co-ordinates. Rogers gave me the same co-ordinates but, sir, Mr. Spock *wasn't* there. What should we do now?"

"Send the others out to search for him," Kirk said. "His hood is green and yellow, isn't it?"

"Aye, sir," Dawson replied.

"He should be easy to spot, then. You stay at the inn as liaison. I'm going to the transporter room to see if something is wrong with the locator board. If it's not malfunctioning, I'll be down shortly to direct search operations. Kirk out."

Dawson faded off the main screen. Kirk's inner worry didn't show on his face as he rose swiftly from his command chair. He strained to keep his emotional responses bottled up at all times; so, for the benefit of those around him, he seemed to meet even the most desperate situation with an air of confident composure. That's why Kirk so enjoyed his occasional hours with Dr. McCoy, when he could unbend and become a mere human.

"Sulu, take the con. I'll be in Transporter Room One, if you need me. McCoy, come with me."

When Kirk and McCoy entered the transporter room, it seemed empty. The circular transporter stage with its six personnel plates was on his left. The main control console was to his right and ahead of him. From a door in a niche next to the transporter stage, he heard a familiar Scots' burr.

"It canna be!"

"What can't, Scotty?" Kirk asked, stepping up to the compartment where much of the transporter's equipment was.

Scott and Rogers looked up from a partially disassembled electronic module.

"Look," Scott said, pointing to a junction box. "Someone has tinkered with the locator circuit tuned to Mr. Spock's communicator in such a way that the readout on the board seems perfectly normal. That shunt, there, and the one right next to it," he pointed to two tiny connections with his synchronic meter, "give a coordinate readout on the board that looks perfectly normal, but actually the tight beam connection between the ship and the communicator has been cut. It's a braw piece o' work. We'd have had nae reason to suspect anything was wrong if Mr. Dawson hadnae checked the co-ordinates and found nae'an there. But why would anybody want us to think Mr. Spock was in one place when actually he was someplace else?"

"I wonder if . . ." The transporter officer's voice trailed off and he shook his head. "No, that doesn't make sense, either."

"What?" Kirk demanded.

"Yeoman Jenkins was on duty here the night before last. He mentioned that Mr. Spock came in about oh-two-hundred, and sent him to check something in the Jeffries tube—the tight beam antenna, that was it. Anyway, when Jenkins came back, about a half-hour later, he found Mr. Spock gone. It seemed strange to him that Mr. Spock would leave the station unmanned, even though no one was down at Kyros at the time. He was bothered by it and by Mr. Spock's manner. He said there was something almost furtive about it." Rogers fell silent.

"Well, whatever his problem is, we've got to get him up here at once," Kirk said. "But before we can do that, we have to find out where he is. Scotty, how long before you can straighten out the locator circuit and get Spock's co-ordinates?"

For an answer, Scott put down the synchronic meter, removed a small disassembler from a repair kit, and removed the shunt.

"Ready now, sir," he said. "We'll snap this module

back in the locator board an' have the answer in a second." He picked up the component gently, carried it to the transporter room console, crawled underneath the console, and replaced the unit. He replaced the inspection plate, came out from under, pressed a button for a circuit tester and nodded in satisfaction as green lights appeared.

"Now we'll find him," Scott said. He checked a display for the communicator frequency assigned to Spock. "If it were anyone else but our Vulcan friend, I'd guess he had a lassie down there and didna want us to ken where he was, during his more loving moments. It must be sair hard to mate once every seven years. Whatever his reasons were for his tinkering, if it was he, they weren't the usual ones."

"The co-ordinates, if you please, Mr. Scott," Kirk demanded impatiently.

"Coming up, sir," Scott said. He pressed a button.

The locator board remained black.

"I thought you had the circuit straightened out!" Kirk said.

Scott swore softly and his fingers punched button after button. The green lights continued to come on. Finally, the engineer threw up his hands in baffled discouragement.

"Well, Scotty?" Kirk asked.

"It's no good, sir. The circuits are all right, but Mr. Spock has vanished!"

CHAPTER THREE

"That tears it," Scott murmured. "You can see for yourself, sir, Mr. Spock is gone. Where, I dinna ken, but gone he is."

"At the least, the locator circuit on his communicator isn't responding to our signal," Kirk said. He thought for a moment. "I wonder if that radiation front could be interfering with our locating frequencies?"

"I'll check," Scott said. "We'll see if Dawson's communicator is responding." He fed its frequency into the locator and pressed a button. Instantly, a series of bright green numerals appeared on the screen set in the face of the console.

"We're getting through, at least," Kirk said. "Check those against Dawson's location."

Scott nodded and bent over the console. A second later, a map of the city of Andros appeared on the viewing screen, a grid superimposed on it. When Dawson's co-ordinates were compared against where the board said he was, a bright blip appeared in the exact center of a circled location.

"They check, sir," Scott said. "That readout shows that Dawson is at the inn, and that's where he's supposed to be."

Kirk took a long moment before replying. When he did, he spoke carefully. "Since the locator is working properly, Spock is either dead, unconscious, or he's tampered with the communicator's locator circuit. Considering the tinkering that was done up here, it seems likely he's modified his communicator. But . . . why?"

"Now, Captain," Scott said. "We're not *sure* he altered the board. And what's mair, it's humanly impossible for a communicator to be tampered with, with what Mr. Spock has available to him down there."

"He could have done it up here," McCoy said.

"But, Doctor, a man's communicator is his only link with the ship when he's planet-side. It'd be crazy to disable the locator circuit."

"Spock isn't human," Kirk observed dryly. "He can do almost anything he wants to and, in this case, it seems as though he doesn't want us to find him." He turned to McCoy. "Bones, why? That's your department. Do you have any idea why Spock wouldn't want his location known?"

"It might have something to do with his not beaming up with the rest last night," McCoy answered. "And then again, it might not. I should give up trying to figure out what makes Spock tick, I've tried long enough. He's always taken care to keep the human side he inherited from his mother suppressed. It's true that he always acts logically, but it's usually such an alien logic that much of the time I don't understand *why* he does what he does—unless he cares to explain, that is. When he does, his actions always make perfect sense. When he doesn't, the man's an enigma. Maybe that's what makes him so attractive to women. They find him 'fascinating,' " McCoy finished.

"Could his implant have anything to do with this?"

McCoy shook his head. "I don't see how. When Spock came to sickbay to get his implant, Ensign George and I checked the profiles carefully and picked the one with the lowest emotional quotient. Even though he knew some of his dop's emotion would come through the link, Spock said it was no problem."

"Couldn't you have altered the device to screen out all emotional input?" Kirk asked.

"Sure," McCoy replied, "but then we would have defeated one of the most important purposes for using it, perfect mimicry of native behavior. Vulcans always react logically to events. With humans and Kyrosians, there's an inevitable emotional component. Eliminate that, and you'll start to call attention to yourself as someone odd and different—which is the last thing we want to happen to a survey party member who's trying to pass as a native!"

McCoy went on, "Spock's dop is a very proper, very respectable, and very unemotional merchant who owns a small pottery shop. There's absolutely nothing in his profile to explain Spock's present behavior. I picked it myself and Sara fed it in."

"Then I guess we'll have to assume that we have a normal Spock who has some good reason for getting himself lost," Kirk said. "But when he returns, he'd better have a very logical explanation for his behavior. We can't wait around here indefinitely. At the rate that radiation is peaking, I've got to get the *Enterprise* out of here before too long. I won't endanger this ship because of some private whim of my first officer."

Kirk paced the floor of the transporter room. "He knows something has happened to make us send out an emergency recall." He paused suddenly. "Or does he? Bones, what if the tingler doesn't work on a Vulcan? If he never received our message, he'd have no way of knowing that he'd have to cut short whatever he's up to. He'd never disobey a direct order, no matter how important his project was."

"It's as you said before, Jim," McCoy said grimly. "If he's dead . . . but if he's alive, he got the signal. There may be a lot of anatomical differences between humans and Vulcans—Spock's heart being where his liver ought to be, among others—but a nerve is a nerve to both of us."

"He could be a prisoner . . ." Scott said.

"We've got to know for sure," Kirk said. "Scotty, is there anyway you could lock onto Spock's tricorder? He took it with him."

"Negative, sir," replied the engineering officer. "A tricorder is too well shielded. There's nae enou' energy leakage to get a fix."

"There has to be a way . . ." Kirk muttered, clenching his fists and resuming his anxious pacing of the transporter room.

As if on cue, the communicator on the transporter console bleeped, signaling a call from the survey party. Scott reached toward the board, but Kirk, who was a bit closer, jabbed down a finger.

"Kirk here. Any word of Spock?"

"Yes, sir." Dawson's voice sounded strained. "I think you'd better beam us up at once."

"Is he with you?"

"No, sir, he—"

"Then do you know where he is?" Kirk interrupted.

"No, sir, but he sent a message. It's addressed to you, Captain."

"Well, he's alive anyway. Bring 'em up, Scotty."

The engineer stepped to the board and placed his thick fingers on the phase controls. Moving them gently, he pushed them along the runner slots. A deep hum of power filled the transporter room, and, after a few seconds, as the hum built up, the shimmering effect of the transporter's carrier wave appeared over five of the six circular plates on the stage. Five figures in Kyrosian dress stepped down. One of them approached Kirk and handed him a scroll tied with a brightly colored ribbon.

"Mr. Spock's message, sir. An old beggar woman brought it to me at the inn."

Kirk glanced at the parchment-like scroll. It was from Spock all right. Kirk's name was written on the outside in lettering so precise that it could have been printed by a computer.

As Kirk untied the ribbon and opened the scroll, Scott watched as Dawson removed his garishly marked, close-fitting hood, displaying his newly-shaven head.

"What were you doing down there, Lieutenant? Playing trick or treat?"

Dawson grinned and rubbed his head. "My dop is a hillman, Commander. At least he was before he got kicked out of his clan for propositioning one of the chief's wives. Andros is full of hillmen who have had their hoods lifted."

"Who *what?*" Scott asked.

"Had their hoods lifted. Exposing the face is as taboo among the hill tribes as exposing the breasts once was back on Earth a few hundred years ago. On Kyros, once your face has been seen by an enemy, you're wide open to any spell he wants to send your way. The worst punishment a clan can inflict on an erring member, aside from killing him, is to strip off his hood in public. Once his features are known, he usually would opt for immediate, permanent, self-imposed exile. Or commit suicide. Most of them get to Andros and live together in a slum, since no hill tribe will take a reject from another . . ."

Kirk's voice suddenly halted further conversation. His face a frozen mask, he spoke in unnaturally calm, precise tones.

"Mr. Scott, please call the warp drive engine room and have your people check the status of the trilithium modulator crystals in the field damper circuits. Have them check stores to see if the replacements are there."

"Now why would you be wanting the trilithium modules checked at a time like this?"

"Please carry out my orders, Mr. Scott," Kirk said. Although he gave no hint of his inner turmoil, there was a quality to his voice that made Scott jump.

"Aye, aye, sir."

"Jim, what the hell's wrong?" McCoy asked. Kirk ignored him, staring at the scroll held in his hands.

Scott went to the communicator and began to snap orders to the duty officers in the warp drive engineering room. When they replied, their voices were high and excited. Scott turned to his captain, his broad face ashen.

"They're gone! The replacements, too! Our warp drive is disabled!"

"Then Spock wasn't bluffing," Kirk said in a low voice. His steady eyes looked first at his engineering officer and then at the ship's surgeon.

"Gentlemen," he continued in the same slow, measured tones, "I regret to inform you that the *Enterprise* and her crew are at the mercy of a madman. Mr. Spock has gone insane."

His face expressionless, he began to read aloud from the parchment-like scroll while his officers stared at him in shock.

Stardate 6718.1
Captain Kirk:

No longer the void. No longer the frigid wanderings through empty corridors of self. I have been touched. I have been annointed. I have seen.

There are gods, and they move in mysterious ways; and the strangest of these is that they should select a poor human-Vulcan hybrid as the agent through which their will is to be done. Kyros reeks with sin; flame and sword shall cleanse it, though persuasion is the first commandment. First, Andros, and then, as my forces grow, city after city until the whole planet is united into one people governed by the divine law.

You will say that in doing this I am violating General Order Number One. So be it. I obey a higher law. I realize that you, who have not been touched by the light, will feel compelled to use your resources to attempt to thwart my mission.

I do not underestimate the mighty forces the Enterprise *can bring to bear. I have therefore taken steps to ensure that you and your ship remain neutral in the coming struggle between good and evil. I have disabled the warp drive by removing the trilithium modulator crystals from the field damper circuits. These I have placed in my tricorder. I have altered its circuits in such a way that any manifestation of phaser energy or communicator frequencies will result in their immediate destruction.*

It may be that once Kyros is purged, the gods will wish to use the Enterprise *to bring the light to other systems. Their will in this matter has not yet been revealed to me. For the moment, you will remain in orbit and be prepared to render such assistance to my mission as I and the gods deem necessary.*

That which the gods have ordained must come to pass. Be happy that you have been granted a small place in the carrying out of their will.

Let there be peace between us,
The Messiah (once known as Spock).

When Kirk finished reading, he raised his eyes slowly, saying quietly, "We have a problem, gentlemen. Please have all department heads meet me in the brief-

ing room in five minutes." With that, he turned and
left the transporter room, his thoughts boiling with worry and fear for the mad Vulcan.

Every seat in the briefing room was occupied when
Kirk entered and took his place at the head of the long
table. Grim faces and worried eyes told that McCoy
and Scott had been unable to keep the news to themselves. Several excited questions were flung at Kirk. He
raised a hand for silence and in slow, measured tones,
began to speak.

"Gentlemen, no problem is incapable of a solution if
approached in a calm, logical way. Our situation isn't
good, but we've been in worse ones and won through
to safety. Let me first make a brief situational analysis,
then we'll consider what is to be done.

"Mr. Scott, am I correct in assuming that with the
modulator crystals gone, the warp drive is inoperable?"

"Aye, sir," Scott replied, almost in tears at what had
been done to his beloved engines. "The crystals are
isotopes of our main drive dilithium crystals, and they
keep the matter/anti-matter damper field stable. Wi'oot
the field, the reaction would go critical in nanoseconds
and there'd be naething left of the *Enterprise* but a
burning ball of plasma!"

"So we're stranded," Kirk said flatly. "And with our
sub-space radio out, there's no way we can summon
help. Mr. Helman, has there been any change in the
forecast of when that front will peak?"

"Only for the worse now, sir," the second science
officer replied, shaking his head somberly. "I checked
the computer not long ago and the probability is now
.98 that radiation will reach one hundred rad by 20:00
hours, eight days from now. Duration estimate, according to the computer, has bottomed out at one month."

Kirk leaned back in his chair and surveyed the
sober-faced officers.

"It would seem then, gentlemen," he said, "that cir-
cumstances limit us to two possible courses of action.
First, we can abandon ship, an action I intend to use
only as a final resort. If we do beam down, we'll never

be able to return to the ship. By the time the storm is over, she will be hopelessly—and permanently—radioactive. Further, if we are faced with abandoning ship, we won't be able to take any of the usual survival gear with us. Since there are no uninhabited lands below, we would shortly be in contact with the native population. Thus, any use of, or display of any of our advanced technology would be a violation of General Order One."

The room was silent as space as Kirk went on. "Therefore, about all we'd be able to take with us are the clothes on our backs—and they'd be Kyrosian clothes, at that—which means there'd be little we could do to resist Spock's plans to dominate Kyros. He obviously intends to disregard General Order One, and his ultimatum implies that he wouldn't scruple to use his vast scientific knowledge. Metallurgy down there is advanced enough to make the production of crude firearms a definite possibility. And finally, to make our situation even worse, it may well be that our last position report never got through to Starfleet because of the sub-space radiation front. Our chances of rescue, then, are exceedingly slim.

"The only alternative we have is to find Spock and retrieve the trilithium modules before our eight days are up. I suggest we proceed to that consideration immediately. Dr. McCoy."

"Yes, sir?"

"Something has obviously gone wrong with Mr. Spock's implant. Will you please review the procedure and the profile of his native link? We might make our job easier that way."

"Certainly, sir," McCoy said. He walked to the computer terminal at the other end of the conference table, sat in front of it and pushed a button. A visual monitor on the bulkhead was revealed behind a sliding panel. He punched another button and the low hum of the activated terminal filled the room.

"Computer . . ." McCoy began.

"Recording."

"I want access to all medical records on the tele-scan project."

"Working."

"Display the profile of Commander Spock's Kyrosian link."

"Working," the computer replied again. A moment later, the monitor screen was filled with the glowing green lines of the Kyrosian personality profile.

McCoy rose partway out of his seat. "My god!" he exploded.

"What's the matter, Bones?" Kirk asked, moving toward the monitor screen.

"That's the profile of a madman! If Spock is hooked into that, no wonder he's acting like he is! But how . . . ?" Regaining a little composure, McCoy reseated himself.

"Computer, scan for error," he demanded in a shaky voice.

"There is no error."

McCoy stared at Kirk.

"Computer," Kirk said, "identify that profile."

The computer began to speak. "Name, Chag Gara. Age, forty-three. Origin, hill clan, Tara. Subject is a paranoid who believes he has been chosen by the tribal gods to lead a crusade to unify Kyros' city-states under a theocratic government with himself as head. Subject has been able to attract a certain following among the unsophisticated, superstitious hill tribes. Probability is that subject induces highly emotional state in listeners. Biographical data in medical banks indicates subject has been in Andros for several weeks attempting to enlist the city-dwellers in his crusade. His low general intelligence and inability to order his thoughts logically have mitigated against the use of the same tactics in Andros which were moderately successful in the hills. Except for a small scattering of unstable urbanites, subject is considered a mentally disturbed fanatic and has been received with hostility and derision. Probability is .87 that subject will resort to military action. The nearest analogs in data banks are: Mohammed, founder Islam, approximately A.D. 600, planet Sol 3; Stur, founder Thirty Tribes, Year of Blood, planet Vulcan; Nerid . . ."

"Stop," Kirk ordered. "Estimate probability of Chag Gara's success."

"Probability is point zero zero zero one seven," the computer replied.

Kirk stared coldly at the chief medical officer.

"Dr. McCoy, I believe an explanation is in order. Why was my first officer linked to an alien lunatic?"

The other didn't seem to hear the question. He sat staring at the profile, his face still registering shock and dismay. "The implications," he muttered, "the implications . . ."

"Implications later," snapped the captain. "I want to know what happened!"

McCoy shook his head in bewilderment. "I haven't the slightest idea. That profile is almost the complete opposite of what we selected for Spock. Somehow, they must have gotten switched and he was tuned to a profile in our reject file."

"How could that have happened?" Kirk demanded, his voice frosty.

"It couldn't have! When Ensign George beamed up with the personality scans she made from the inn, she, Nurse Chapel, and I sorted and cataloged them according to whether they would be suitable or not. We even took physical build into account, because there is a relationship between it and behavior. We stored the rejects in the medical library for future study and then began the matching process. I personally cross-indexed each profile with the survey party member with whom it was going to be linked and placed the mag-cards in the tuner." He gestured toward the screen. "This . . . this is impossible!"

"Impossible or not," Kirk said, "we're faced with a deliberate act of sabotage. I want everyone who had any connection with the telescan project up here on the double. If there has been any violation of Starfleet regulations which has resulted in a violation of General

Order Number One, there's going to be an immediate
court-martial."

McCoy turned to the communicator. On ship-wide
call, he said, "Dr. Mbenga, Nurse Chapel, and Ensign George: report to the briefing room at once."

"I don't think you realize the implications of what
has happened, Captain," McCoy said, facing Kirk.
"Watch. Computer."

"Recording."

"Display Commander Spock's personality profile."

"Working," the computer replied, and a complex
graph replaced that of the Kyrosian hillman.

"Let me explain what this shows about Spock," Mc-
Coy said, once more in control of himself. "We can
ignore most of this," he said, as he gestured to the
complex electronic graph. "Only five areas are of immediate concern. Computer, bar graph the IQ, LQ,
EQ, DQ, and SQ. Wipe the rest."

The screen blanked for a second, then a new configuration appeared.

"Observe, gentlemen," McCoy began, pointing to
the first bar. "Spock's intelligence quotient almost runs
off the scale. He has a high genius rating, higher than
most Vulcans and much higher than humans. His LQ
—logic quotient, that is—which measures his ability to
apply his intelligence to the logical solution of problems, is equally high." He pointed to the second bar.
"The man is an organic computer. Once supplied with
sufficient data, he always arrives at the optimum solution."

"Why the lecture?" Kirk asked. "We know all that."

"You'll see my point in a minute, Captain. In contrast," he pointed again, "his emotional quotient is extremely low. If he were a pure Vulcan, it would be
zero. His DQ is."

"DQ?" asked Kirk.

"Delusional quotient. That's a measurement of the
extent to which personal beliefs interfere with the per-
ception of objective reality. His sensuality quotient, for
obvious reasons of Vulcan physiology, is also zero. Mr.

Spock is incapable of any sexual feelings except for widely spaced periods of intense arousal. And now, to the point. Computer."

"Recording."

"Bar graph the same characteristics of subject Kyrosian Chag Gara."

"Working."

Another graph appeared on the screen.

"You will note here," McCoy said, "a profile that is almost diametrically opposed to our first officer's. Very low IQ, an almost nonexistent LQ, but an abnormally high EQ, DQ, and SQ. From the last, I'd surmise that he preaches a paradise for the faithful that is full of beautiful and eager houris. I'd also bet that he spends as much time chasing women as he does preaching," McCoy concluded.

"I'm afraid to see what's coming next," Kirk said soberly.

In reply, McCoy nodded. He spoke to the computer. "Computer . . . superimpose Spock's graph on the one now showing."

There was a collective gasp from the somber group as the new image appeared. Each of the five bars reached almost to the top of the scale.

"And that, gentlemen, is what we're up against. Spock is locked into a delusional syndrome from which he can't escape. He *knows* the gods have chosen him as an instrument of their will, and he will apply all of his vast intellectual resources to carry it out. Unless we stop him before his movement acquires momentum, his hordes will sweep across Kyros converting or killing."

Kirk smashed his fist down on the desk.

"You assured me the implants were foolproof! You said you checked Spock carefully!" he said to McCoy accusingly.

"They are, when used properly, Captain," McCoy replied defensively. "But they were never designed for a match-up like this. At the moment of linkage between Spock and Gara, there must have been an emotional surge that blew the input filter stage. In that instant, that delusional pattern was imprinted on Spock's brain,

and he knew himself to be the chosen of the gods."
McCoy paused for a moment and glanced at the assembled men and women.

"It wasn't our first officer who was prowling the ship the night before last. It was the Messiah!"

CHAPTER FOUR

Dr. Mbenga, a graying, stocky black; Lieutenant Christine Chapel, a tall, willowy blonde; and Ensign Sara George, a small, shapely woman with a long fall of lustrous black hair, were waiting in the corridor outside of the briefing room. As the door hissed open and the sober-faced officers filed out, Kirk beckoned the three in. Once McCoy's staff was seated at the conference table, Kirk quickly outlined the happenings of the past hour.

". . . and one of you," he concluded coldly, "has not only placed the *Enterprise* in extreme jeopardy, but has turned a mad wolf loose in a fold of defenseless sheep. General Order One is explicit; no action may be taken by any agent of Starfleet Command which can in any way affect the normal development of an alien planet. Although we may not approve of the institutions of a native society, we have no right to intervene and direct history in the way we feel it should go. Earth's own past is a tragic record of the consequences of a technologically advanced culture imposing its values and life-style on less advanced people. There would be no question in the mind of any board of inquiry that, as a consequence of the *Enterprise*'s visit and of the action of one of you, a force has been released on Kyros which threatens to transform the planet into an ugly theocratic state ruled by a mad genius. The ship's department heads will reconvene shortly to try to arrive at a course of action. In the meantime, I'm going to find out which of you is responsible for transforming my first officer into a madman. Dr. Mbenga, we'll start with you. Please describe your role in the programming."

The scholarly black frowned, looked at Kirk

thoughtfully and said, "I'm afraid I can't be of much help. I had nothing to do with program selection and the subsequent telepathic linkage. I'm a surgeon, Captain. I prepared the patients by drilling a small cavity in the right mastoid behind the ear. Once Dr. McCoy had tuned the implant to a particular native profile, inserted it, then checked to see that a telepathic link had been established, I performed the necessary microsurgery to close the incision. That was the extent of my involvement."

"He's right, Jim," McCoy said. "I had Nurse Chapel supervise the actual programming."

"Christine?" Kirk asked.

The attractive blonde nurse cast a nervous glance at Ensign George, who returned the look with one of disdain. She faced Kirk, seemingly on the verge of tears. "I did do the profile feed-ins, Captain," she began in a choked voice, "but each time I checked the profile print-out on the mag-card to be sure there was no mistake on the matching. I . . . I was . . . es . . . especially careful when Mr. Spock's turn came. Dr. McCoy . . . understands why . . ." she glanced appealingly at the chief surgeon.

He nodded sympathetically. Like many female crew members aboard the starship, Lieutenant Chapel was hopelessly in love with the tall, handsome Vulcan. She was a sensible woman, though, and knew that any relationship other than a purely professional one was impossible. But every time he came near her, a wave of desire washed through her that she found hard to control, but did . . . somehow.

"I . . . I wouldn't do anything to harm Mr. Spock. I've had enough tragedy in my life," she went on, referring to her years' long search for a man she had once loved who had been lost on a space expedition, and the heartbreak and horror that came when she finally found him.*

Kirk considered the woman's words. As he looked

*See: *"What Are Little Girls Made Of?"* STAR TREK 11, Bantam Books, 1975.

into her strained and worried face, he thought: True, but infatuation can make the best of us do strange things. Could she have hoped that linkage with a highly emotional Kyrosian mind would make Spock react to her femininity in human terms? Kirk rejected that thought almost as soon as it entered his mind. She would be no more capable of doing that than McCoy would be of administering an aphrodisiac to a woman he desired.

And that left only the petite newcomer, Ensign George. Though she had a pertly attractive face and a provocatively rounded body, the few brief contacts Kirk had had with her since she joined the *Enterprise* had given him the impression of a person so involved in her work that there was no place for anything else. But now, as she looked at him, there was a new quality about her, a smoldering sensuality that Kirk's maleness couldn't help reacting to.

"Well, Ensign?" Kirk said.

"I had nothing to do with whatever happened to Mr. Spock," she said defiantly. "Somehow, the mag-cards must have gotten mixed up. I wasn't even in the operating room when the link was activated."

"More than a mix-up is involved here," Kirk said coldly. "Someone took Chag Gara's profile from the medical library, wiped the one that had been originally selected for Spock, and deliberately imprinted Gara's personality pattern. Since the visual identification printout on the card was that of the original subject, neither Dr. McCoy nor Lieutenant Chapel had any way of knowing that a switch was made."

"You seem to have found me guilty already, Captain," she replied.

"Are you?" Kirk demanded.

The woman's composure remained unruffled. "Chapel knows how to run the equipment," she said coolly, "and she knows how to read profiles. Maybe Gara's sensuality quotient gave her a bright idea. Her feelings about Spock are no real secret; she turns into a quivering schoolgirl every time he comes in sight."

Lieutenant Chapel's eyes brimmed with tears at the accusation, but her voice retained a bite as she glared at the smaller woman. "You're lying. You had the opportunity, too, and the motive. I've seen you near Spock . . ." Turning to the men, she said. "You both know I'd never . . . never do anything like that."

"Of course, Christine," McCoy replied softly.

Another five minutes of interrogation brought nothing but continued denials.

"We're getting no place," Kirk said, glancing at the digital chronometer on one bulkhead impatiently, "and we have much more important matters to attend to. Dr. Mbenga, Lieutenant Chapel, you are excused. Ensign George, consider yourself under arrest. You will remain in your quarters until a board of court-martial can be convened."

The girl shrugged and started to rise.

"I think we've overlooked something important," McCoy said, making a restraining gesture. "With your permission, Captain, I think I may be able to clear this matter up in a few minutes."

Kirk glanced at the chronometer again, then gave a nod.

"Dr. Mbenga," McCoy directed, "will you please go to sickbay and get me a spray hypo of 200 milligrams of neo-chlorprothixene."

As the black physician left, Kirk looked at McCoy with a puzzled expression.

"What's all this?"

"I've been working quite closely with Sara the last few weeks, but she hasn't been the same person since she received her dop," McCoy replied. "Until now, I thought the dop effect was only minor, but her behavior during the last half hour indicates a major change. Her dop's behavior pattern must be so different from her own that a major psychic distortion has taken place. I'm going to inject her with a fast-acting ataractic—"

"A what?"

"Ataractic. It's a powerful tranquilizer that will temporarily depress the substrates of the midbrain that

control emotional responses. My hunch is that once
Sara is her normal cool, cerebral self, she'll be able to
tell us what happened."

At his words, Ensign George stood up. Idly, she
wandered toward the briefing room door just as Dr.
Mbenga came in to hand McCoy the hypo. She
slammed into him, trying to get out.

"Grab her!" McCoy shouted.

Kirk jumped, throwing his arms about her. She
struggled fiercely, clawing and screaming. McCoy
dashed to her side, slapped the end of the hypo against
her arm and pressed. There was a low hiss as the spray
penetrated to her skin. Kirk held onto her as she stiffened, then collapsed.

"Put her in that chair, Jim," McCoy said. "She isn't
unconscious, but she isn't able to stand by herself."

As the two officers stood looking down at her, the
girl's face began to change. The look of sullen defiance
drained away to be replaced by an expressionless mask.

"All right, Sara," McCoy said, "how did it happen?"

When she answered, her voice was as flat and tone-
less as the ship's computer.

"My life has always been my work; I refused to allow myself to get entangled in emotional relationships.
I considered them disruptive and counterproductive.
When I met Mr. Spock, all that changed. I found him
strangely attractive. I was conscious of his maleness—
something that never happened to me before—but I
controlled that easily. I was determined to let nothing
interfere with my work. But when I beamed up with
that batch of native profiles and checked through them,
I found one so unlike my own that I was filled with an
intense curiosity. I wondered what it would be like to
be that person, to feel the way she felt. For once in my
life I gave in to temptation and acted on impulse. At
any rate, I tuned my telescan link to that profile and let
it be implanted. Since I was in charge of that much of
the experiment, they didn't think to check on the one I
chose. Dr. McCoy and the rest assumed I would follow
normal procedure."

The woman, in spite of the drug, squirmed in her seat.

"The instant the linkage was established," she said, "I knew I had made a terrible mistake. I found myself in the grip of emotional forces I couldn't control. It was too late to do anything about it. From then on, I knew what I was doing, and I hated myself for it, hated those feelings, but I couldn't . . . couldn't stop."

"Can you say why?" McCoy asked softly.

"I think because I had repressed my own emotions for so long, refusing to deal with them, trying only to deny them. When my dop's feelings came surging across. I couldn't handle them," the ensign went on, her voice flat and objective. "When I was assigned to the *Enterprise* and learned of Lieutenant Chapel's feelings about Spock, I thought, how illogical. I had nothing but contempt for her. I couldn't conceive of a mind fine enough to be a Starfleet officer and earn a doctorate in bio-research and medicine, letting itself be disturbed by such a futile hope and childish infatuation. But like Spock, I denied my own humanity. Unlike him, however, I am human, and humans are sexual beings. The ordinary linkage allows just enough emotion to make the observer authentic to a native; but, like Spock, I became my dop. If you will examine her profile you will see."

McCoy gave the necessary commands to the computer, and when the personality profile appeared on the screen, he whistled in astonishment.

"Good Lord, Jim, look at that!"

"You know I can't read those wiggles, Bones," Kirk said. "What does it mean?"

"It means that Sara has hooked herself into a walking sex machine with as many inhibitions as a green Orion slave girl—namely, none! This profile's only purpose in life seems to be immediate and frequent gratification of her desires of the moment." McCoy looked at the woman sprawled in the chair.

"What do you know about her, Sara?"

"Not much. When I was collecting the profiles, I

tried to get as much diversity as possible. She seemed a good candidate because of her beauty and an aura of sexual magnetism around her. As she went through the plaza that day, nearly every male gawked at her. She was obviously lower-class, but I thought her behavioral characteristics might be useful if a mission required a female officer with those characteristics." She paused.

"Go on, Ensign," Kirk prompted.

"Yes, sir," Ensign George replied. "Once the link was established, it wasn't long before I had convinced myself that linking Mr. Spock with an equally emotional native might have the same effect on him as it did on me. Being half-human, his long frigid periods could be as much the result of psychological conditioning as of physiological factors. So I switched profiles."

"And found you were right," McCoy murmured.

"Yes," she confirmed in an unemotional voice. "When we beamed down with the rest of the party that first morning, it just took an exchange of glances to communicate what we both had in mind. As soon as the others left . . ."

"You don't have to go on, Sara," McCoy interrupted.

"Your injection is still blocking my sub-cortical structures, Doctor," she said. "At the moment, I have no feelings about it. It is of clinical interest only."

In spite of her words, she paused. Her face worked slightly, twitching with shame, alternating with a smile.

"We took off our clothes and made love. We were like two rutting cats. My old self looked on in horror and disgust at my body's violation; but my new self reveled in it, craved it, and was satisfied." Her voice lowered as she paused again.

"I would suggest, Captain," she began again after a moment, "that my implant be removed as soon as possible. Otherwise, I will find some way to get back down to Kyros and find Mr. Spock. I want . . ." Her voice suddenly trailed off and she slumped forward.

McCoy made a quick check. "Respiration and pulse normal," he announced. "I gave her a high dose and it's finally hit her central nervous system. No harm done, but she'll be out for an hour or so." McCoy went to the intraship communicator, called sickbay and ordered a stretcher party to the briefing room. As the unconscious woman was borne away a few minutes later, and when the captain and doctor were alone, Kirk turned a shocked face to McCoy.

"Bones, she *had* to be hallucinating! Spock and I have served together for years. He could no more behave in the way she described than he could fly!"

"*Our* Mr. Spock couldn't," McCoy agreed. "The creature that now inhabits his body is a different matter."

The re-convened emergency council had come to an end. Kirk rose from his chair and looked soberly around the conference table.

"It is agreed, then, that since Mr. Spock has disappeared, our only chance is to locate Chag Gara. If we can get him up here, Dr. McCoy assures me that electronically augmented crash psycho-therapy can erase his delusional patterns in hours. Once they stop feeding across the link, Spock will return to normal and, realizing what he has done, rejoin the ship immediately with the trilithium modules."

"Somewhat abashed, I imagine," McCoy said dryly. "It's going to be most interesting to hear him comment on his recent behavior."

"Finding Chag Gara shouldn't be too difficult," Kirk continued. "He's conspicuous, and is unaware of what has been going on. Since his main weakness is women, we'll lure him to the inn with Ensign George. McCoy will inject him and we'll beam up."

Lieutenant Uhura raised her hand. "But Captain," she said, "you told us that Sara admitted she would have one thought in mind when Dr. McCoy's injection wore off; she'd want to get back to Kyros and resume her—" the black officer paused a moment—" 'relationship' with Mr. Spock. How do you expect her to follow your orders and not her new feelings?"

"Good question," Kirk said. "Dr. McCoy will be

working on that problem soon. By removing Ensign George's implant and adding another filter stage, the emotional input from her dop will be reduced to a manageable level. She'll be ready for duty tomorrow morning. At that time, Dr. McCoy, Ensign George, and I will beam down. The rest of you will stand by for any action necessary."

"One last question, Captain," Lieutenant Commander Scott said. "What if things dinna work out as planned? If Spock has those birkies making guns . . ." Scott trailed off, staring at Kirk.

There was a long silence. When Kirk finally answered, his voice was stiff, betraying his strenuous efforts to control his inner anguish.

"If worst comes to worst, Mr. Scott, and we can't stop Spock the way we plan, we must attempt to restore the culture to what it was before we came by excising the infection. By any means."

Kirk surveyed the grim-faced personnel, his own face a frozen mask.

"Dismissed."

CHAPTER FIVE

Captain's log: Stardate 6721.3:

The investigation into Spock's sudden insanity has revealed a disturbing consequence of the cephalic implant experiment.

Feedback from the subconscious of her dop caused Ensign Sara George, one of the members of the survey party, to switch the programming for Commander Spock, giving him an unstable, highly emotional "host."

Dr. McCoy and I are preparing to beam down, search for, and capture the Kyrosian to whom Spock is linked. Ensign George will accompany us, and McCoy feels it will be therapeutic. I do not hold Ensign George responsible for her actions while under the influence of her dop and have ordered her to act as our interpreter and guide since the time involved for McCoy and I to receive implants would consume nearly a day, a day which Kyros cannot afford.

Kirk released the button on the console of the transporter, shutting off the log channel. He was dressed in the uniform of a Kyrosian sea captain from the western islands: knee-length white shorts, sandals, and a vest-like upper garment with a short cape attached to the shoulders. The vest was held shut by a heavy gold chain with a dark blue stone, the symbol of his rank, dangling from a fob. At his waist was a soft, animal-skin pouch containing money in the form of triangularly-cut gold coins. Also at his waist was a short, heavy club.

"Where is Ensign George?" Kirk asked, glancing at McCoy. McCoy, dressed similarly to Kirk except that his chain was made of leather, merely shrugged.

"I just hope we don't get arrested for passing Scotty's funny money," the doctor said, touching his pouch.

"Och, Doctor," Scott retorted from the transporter console. "It's as gude as gold . . . in fact, it is."

Kirk smiled slightly. He approached the wall-mounted communicator and was about to issue a ship-wide call for the ensign, when she walked through the opening doors of the transporter room. Her small, trim figure was wrapped in the chiton-like garment characteristic of Kyrosian women.

"I'm sorry, Captain, I couldn't find my comb." Her hand touched the elaborate comb which rose a full fifteen centimeters above her long, black hair. It curved over her head from ear to ear and a short veil dangled from it, just brushing the nape of her neck.

"Beats me how you could miss it," McCoy muttered.

The woman gave the doctor a grimace, but stepped toward the transporter stage. Kirk turned toward Scott, who waited patiently at the console.

"Are the inn's co-ordinates locked in, Scotty?"

"Aye, Captain," Scott replied crisply.

"Whoops!" McCoy said suddenly, glancing down at the pale hairy legs extending below the cuffs of his shorts.

"What's wrong?" Kirk asked.

"Costume slipping. Unless I only stood night watches, these legs of mine are much too pale for a sea-faring man." McCoy stepped off the transporter stage and hurried out.

A few minutes later, he returned with his skin tinted a deep mahogany brown. "There. Shall we proceed?"

"Have you got the hypo for Gara?" Kirk asked.

"Right here, Jim," McCoy replied, slapping his pouch. "It's loaded with enough pirotoline to knock out a Rigellian mountain devil."

"Good," Kirk said. "When we locate him, and our little sex machine gets him turned on, our problems will be solved. Do you think you'll be able to handle your end, Sara?"

"Yes, sir," she replied, her voice cool and professional. "The new filter stage in my implant is working perfectly. Enough of my dop is coming through so that I can imitate her actions—but with me firmly in control."

"Good girl." Kirk turned to Scott.

"All right," he said to the engineer, "give us an hour. Spock wasn't bluffing, I'm sure, when he said he rigged his tricorder to detect communicators, so we'll be out of contact. We'll have to work on blind coordinates from here on in. Keep the transporter locked onto the inn room and energize every fifteen minutes."

"No problem, Captain," Scott replied.

Kirk turned to face the other two. "That's a fetching ensemble, Doctor, you must introduce me to your couturier," he heard Sara say to McCoy.

"It's what they're wearing this season," McCoy retorted.

"Are you two ready to beam down?" Kirk asked.

"Ready as I'll ever be, Jim," McCoy replied unhappily. "I trust that what comes out down there bears some resemblance to what went in." He glanced ruefully at his legs again. "Those knees may be knobby, but at least they're mine."

"With Scotty at the controls, you have nothing to worry about."

"The last time he was at the controls, we ended up with duplicate Spocks," McCoy said sourly.*

"This time," Kirk said, as he stepped onto the transporter, "I'll settle for just one. All right, Mr. Scott, energize."

"Energizing, sir," responded Scott. His thick fingers played over the controls, then gripped the phasing runners. The deep hum of power from the operating transporter filled the room, and the rising crackle of the carrier wave became more distinct.

The *Enterprise* began to fade from Kirk's sight. He caught a glimpse of a darkened room with a single, glowing lamp. Then suddenly, the ship was back and solid around him.

"What's the problem, Scotty?"

_____

*See: SPOCK MUST DIE!, Bantam Books, 1970.

"Och! That damn radiation must be bollixing up the magnetic field of the planet and reflecting back the transporter beam."

He worked the controls to compensate for the effects of the slowly increasing radiation front.

"Captain, if this interference keeps building up, an' I ken it will, this transporter is nae going to be working at her best. None of them will." He looked at his captain with a grim face. "I canna guarantee I'll be able to bring you back."

Kirk glanced at McCoy, and then George; she gave a slight shrug.

"We'll try to be quick about it, Scotty," Kirk said in a reassuring voice. "Energize, again."

"Aye," Scott said. He looked glum as he moved the phase controls a second time. The power hum resurged, and the *Enterprise* again faded from Kirk's sight. It flickered once, then twice, then once more, before it finally disappeared.

Kirk watched as the darkened room solidified around him again. There was that seemingly interminable moment before it stabilized; then it did, and Kirk knew he was whole and could move. He stepped forward into the weak pool of light cast by a smelly lamp atop a smooth-surfaced table. The lamp held animal fat in an earthen cup with a lit wick floating in it. There were deep shadows in the corners of the room, and the ceiling was black as space itself.

Ensign George went to the room's only window and jerked back the heavy curtain covering it.

The early morning light of Kyr, the system's yellow sun, poured in through mica-like panes set in the frame. Kirk and McCoy crowded close as the woman swung the window open. From their second-story vantage point they looked down on a large, paved plaza, obviously a marketplace from the bustle of activity around the stands and shops that lined it. The plaza was bounded on the left by the city's wall. A main gate, a massive triangular opening with a center post holding the hinges and long ropes running from the base angles to huge winches, gave access to the world beyond. On each side of the gate, steps went up to a parapet that ran along the top of the wall. To the left, and on the far side of the plaza, were numerous multi-level buildings made of stone with sides painted in abstract, geometric shapes.

Ensign George pointed to a raised stone platform near a central well.

"That's a speaker's block," she said. "One of the nice things about Andros is that anybody who wants to can get up there and speak his mind anytime on anything. Chag Gara was up there ranting the day I came down. Only a few people were listening, and most of them were laughing, but I scanned him so I could include some hillmen." Her face grew bleak. "That was my next biggest mistake. If only I—"

"We've no time for 'if onlys,'" Kirk said. "What's our first step?"

Sara took a moment to answer. "Gara usually shows up early. He's a tall, slender man, built much like Commander Spock. He'll be easy to spot. He always wears a black hood with vermilion stripes under the eye slits."

She stepped away from the window. "Once he shows up, I'll have him hooked in no time. My dop knows how to get any man. I'll bring him up the back way, and when you hear us in the hall, get set. Wish me luck," she finished.

She gave them both a languid, promising smile, and her firm bottom gave a provocative wiggle as she slipped out of the door.

An hour crawled by before McCoy called excitedly, "Jim, I think I've spotted our man!"

Kirk jumped up from the bed where he had sprawled and looked out the window.

"Where?"

"There! Coming across the far corner toward the speaker's block."

Kirk followed McCoy's pointing finger.

A small, disciplined group of hillmen was opening a path through a small gathering of curious onlookers. In

their center, head bowed as if in meditation, walked a
man in a long black robe, face hidden behind a red
and black hill mask.

"Where's Sara?" Kirk wondered.

"Over there. She's coming toward him."

The two watched intently. Distant as she was from
the inn, the woman was easy to follow because of the
glittering gold comb in her hair.

"Chag Gara's bodyguard may present a problem,"
Kirk muttered.

"Sara will find a way," McCoy said. "She's as bright
as she is sexy."

As they watched, she made her way through the
ranks of the hillmen and approached the hooded leader,
hands raised as if in supplication. He didn't seem to
notice her as, head bowed, he continued to walk slowly
toward the rostrum. She tugged the sleeve of his flowing robe and he looked at her.

The result was electric!

The robed man jumped back as if he'd seen a veno-
mous snake and, pointing an accusing arm at the woman, shouted something. Two of his hill disciples
grabbed her roughly as he leaped onto the rostrum in
two bounds. He began a rapid, intense scanning of the
faces in the small group of city people who waited to
hear him speak. Then he turned, jumped lithely down
from the stone platform, and began running to the far
side of the square. The people in the crowd looked at
each other with puzzled expressions, and the bodyguard, after several moments of confusion, ran after
him as he disappeared into a narrow alley. The two
holding Sara waited a moment, then pushed her
roughly to the ground and ran off after their companions.

Kirk threw open the door as Sara came running up
the ramp that led to the second story of the inn, then
slammed and barred it as soon as she entered.

"What happened out there?" he demanded angrily.

"I don't know," she said breathlessly. "Those eyes

. . . cold, deadly-looking . . ." Shoulders shaking, she tried to muffle a sob.

McCoy gripped her shoulder firmly. "Stop it, Sara, you're safe here."

A moment later, she was back in control.

"Sorry, my dop . . ." she said in a shaky voice. "I felt it myself, though. I couldn't help it. When he turned to look at me, those red eyes in those narrow slits became . . . horrible! He couldn't have reacted more violently if I'd been lunging at him with a dagger! But why? I used all my dop's wiles. His response doesn't make sense. The Chag Gara I profiled would have responded with a wink and a suggestion to meet somewhere."

Kirk went to the window and stood there for a moment, staring out into Andros.

"Yesterday and the day before—did you have any contact with him that might explain his reaction?" Kirk asked.

"Negative, sir," Sara said to his back. "We never even spoke. After I finished snapping him from here, I went out to get more profiles from other parts of the city. I paused by the platform as he was speaking— ranting, really, about the wickedness of the cities and the wrath of the gods that would follow. There was an almost hypnotic quality about his voice, but he jumped from one idea to another so incoherently it was pathetic. I only stayed a minute or two, so I don't see how he could remember me as anything but another face in the crowd."

Kirk turned away from the window. "Bones, do you get the same reading I do?"

The surgeon nodded somberly. "I'm afraid so, Jim."

"What do you mean?" Sara asked in a puzzled voice.

"Since, as you say, there could be no reason Chag Gara would remember you, then the man in the mask must have been someone else," Kirk said. "Someone who knows you on sight and who could scan that crowd for other faces from the *Enterprise!*"

"Commander Spock!" George gasped.

"Exactly," McCoy said.

"Yes," Kirk muttered. "He's assumed Chag Gara's identity. Spock's brilliance linked to that hill maniac's emotional power, believing, as Chag Gara did, that he's the chosen of the gods . . . destined to bring a new order to Kyros." Kirk paced the small room. "There'll be no laughter when he speaks now. He'll mold his listeners to his will in a way that will make . . . Hitler look like a rank amateur."

"He knows we're down here now, Jim," McCoy said quietly. "What do you think he'll do?"

"Do?" Kirk faced the doctor. "The first thing he'll do —the logical thing—will be to protect his rear, like any good strategist. He'll protect Chag Gara! He can't afford to let us get to him because if we do, he'll lose his emotional power. He's paranoid, thinks he's being persecuted, and we've given him evidence that people are after him. In a warped way, Spock is a whole man for the first time; and now that he's tasted the life he can have—power, women, fame—he won't give it up for the loneliness of a life where the high point of the week was a game of chess with a computer."

"So he'll head for Chag Gara," McCoy said, "to get him before we do."

"Right!" Kirk said smashing a fist into one palm. "We'd better get moving. Sara!"

"Yes, sir?"

"You'll have to take the con. McCoy and I don't know the language or customs and now there's even less time to get implanted. Our disguises as foreign seamen will give us freedom of movement, but we'll only be able to tag along. You'll have to find out where Chag Gara lives, and fast."

"I'll do my best, sir," she said. "What's the procedure if we do find him? Do we try to use me again?"

Kirk thought for a moment then shook his head. "No, that's too uncertain. Chag might agree, but put the rendezvous with you off until later in the day, which might give Spock time to get to him, if he isn't there already. Bones, can you adjust that hypo to give Gara a dose to put him under control without knocking him out?"

"Yes," McCoy replied as he withdrew the hypo from his pouch and made an adjustment. "If I can get close enough to hit him with this, he'll still be able to navigate, but won't know what's going on. We can pass him off as a friend who's had one too many."

"Good," Kirk said, unbarring the door. "Let's move. Sara, even though you didn't intend to, you got us into this mess. Now, it's up to you to help get us out."

CHAPTER SIX

"Follow me, Captain, Doctor," Sara said, turning right as they left the room. "We'll go down the back way."

She led the way through a narrow, gloomy corridor. A few lamps guttered along the walls, throwing a dim, yellowish light. They came to a down-sloping ramp and took it. At the bottom, they exited through swinging doors and found themselves under a portico roof which shielded a patio paved with multi-colored, triangularly-cut stones. Cages holding small, hissing, lizard-like birds hung from brackets attached to the columns which supported the roof.

"This way," the female officer said, and turned to her left. They walked alongside the inn until they came to the end of the building.

Kirk and McCoy at her heels, Sara stepped out into a narrow alley, again turning left. It was like walking along the bottom of an air shaft. Tall buildings on the left, and the high city wall on the right, cut off most of the light and air. A stench rose from the containers of garbage stacked beside rear exits.

When they finally emerged into the square, it was like leaving a dark tunnel. They found themselves squinting and blinking as their eyes adjusted to the bright sunlight.

The woman hesitated for a moment, scanning the crowded square; then she started for the opposite side.

More Kyrosians had begun to congregate in the plaza as Kyr mounted higher in the sky. City women with market baskets were jostled by hooded hillmen stooped under great bundles of hides and bales of a wool-like material brought to the city for barter. Bareheaded farmers in sun-faded smocks carried trays of exotically colored fruits and vegetables. There was a creaking of ungreased wheels as several wagons came through the open, triangular main gate. The tailless, hairless, reptile-like draft animals that were pulling them squealed in protest at the weight of the piles of iron ingots the wagons carried. Behind them came another wagon, a long, eight-wheeled hybrid that was articulated in the middle and had an open wagon in front and a closed van behind.

"Beshwa," Sara said in answer to Kirk's question. "They must have come in to load up with trade goods before they make their summer sweep through the hills."

When they reached the far side of the square, Sara tugged at Kirk's vest-like jacket and gestured toward a stooped, wizened old man standing in front of a shop staring apathetically at a table covered with pottery.

"What about him?" Kirk asked.

"That's the dop I was supposed to link Mr. Spock to," she said bitterly, her voice heavy with self-recrimination. "If I—"

"Right," McCoy interrupted before she could finish, "but there's nothing that can be done about it now. We've got to get to Chag-whatever-his-name-is before Spock does. Now, let's move it, Ensign."

Sara grinned wryly at him and nodded. "I think we should try Vembe's place first. The hillmen don't like city food and a lot of those who have businesses in the plaza eat at his place."

She led them through an archway into a long arcade that stretched along the entire width of the far side of the square. It was lined with many small shops and eating houses. As Sara paused about a third of the way along, McCoy gave an appreciative sniff.

"Something smells good," he said. "I was in such a hurry this morning that I didn't have time for any breakfast." He was turning into the doorway from which came the mouth-watering aroma of roasting meat simmering in some spicy sauce when the girl grabbed his hand.

"Next door," she said, and led the way into a dark

opening that was so low that, small as she was, she had
to stoop to enter.

"Good lord!" muttered McCoy as his nostrils were
assaulted by a charnel stench. "What's that?"

Sara giggled. *"Vris.* It's a hill delicacy. First you take
a haunch of neelot and hang it in a dark room until it's
good and moldy. Then—"

"Neelot?" interrupted McCoy.

"They're those big, hairless, lizard-like animals you
saw pulling carts. They remind me of a skinned manx
cat. The hillmen use them for food, leather, and as
draft animals. There's also a special breed for riding."

"They sound like the old Mongol hordes of Earth
and their horses," Kirk said.

"Never saw a horse—or a cat—with a head like an
alligator," McCoy murmured.

Sara continued to speak to Kirk. "The hill culture is
similar: nomadic people, sparse grazing lands, and a
horse-like animal."

She advanced into the dimly lit interior of Vembe's
eating house and approached a gnarled little man squatting in front of a fire pit. His leather mask was black,
but with orange stripes under the eye slits. Several hillmen glanced at the three, then turned back to their
bowls of vris and jugs of wine.

"Vembe," Sara said and made an odd little bow of
greeting.

The Kyrosian hunched his shoulders in acknowl-
edgment of her salute and, picking up a small pitcher,
dribbled a slimy-looking sauce over the chunks of
greenish-yellow meat that were slowly turning on a spit.
As drops of sauce dripped onto the hot coals, little
puffs of oily smoke arose, and the stench intensified.
Vembe leaned forward, took a long sniff, nodded, and
said something to Sara.

"The *vris* is ready," she translated. "He says he
would be honored if you'd have some."

Kirk's gorge heaved at the thought.

"You can tell him . . . tell him we appreciate the
offer but we both had a very large breakfast before

leaving our ship . . ." Kirk paused, and glanced at McCoy. "Though perhaps I shouldn't speak for the doctor. He was just telling us how hungry he was."

McCoy rolled his eyes and said hastily, "I've a better idea. Tell him our religion won't let us eat meat on whatever day this is."

Sara spoke rapidly to the little man in guttural Kyrosian. Then, gesturing toward her companions, she made what was obviously an introduction. Vembe rose, touched a finger to the middle of his forehead, and bowed. Kirk and McCoy responded with like movements.

"Ask him if he can tell us where to find Chag Gara," Kirk said.

There was a rapid exchange.

"He wants to know what you want with that *zreel.* That's a local insect, a blood-sucker similar to the terrestrial louse," Sara said.

The little man added something in a hostile voice and spat into the fire pit.

"He says that Chag Gara used to be just crazy, but that all of a sudden he's become dangerous. Now, people listen to his ravings and become converted. And that's bad for business," Sara translated.

"Ask him why."

Vembe responded at length, pointing indignantly to the turning joints of neelot.

"He says that if the Messiah goes marching off on a holy war, most of his customers will go along. And that would mean that the best *vris* house in Andros would have to close its doors."

"A gastronomic catastrophe," McCoy muttered, wrinkling his nose.

"De gustibus no disputandem," Kirk said with a grin.

"What does that mean?" Sara asked.

" 'Of taste there is no disputing.' It's an old language, Latin. But let's get back to the business at hand. Vembe is obviously no friend of Gara's. Tell him that Chag committed a horrible crime in our home country and is under sentence of death by torture. Tell him we've journeyed many months over the seas to carry out the sentence, but we can't until we find him."

The woman made a quick translation. When she finished, the old hillman gave a grunt of satisfaction, started to speak, then halted. He stared down into the fire pit for a moment and then cocked his head, muttering something.

"What's he saying?" Kirk demanded impatiently.

"I think he's putting the bite on us. He says he's getting old and his memory isn't what it used to be."

Kirk took the pouch of Kryosian coins from his belt and handed it to the woman.

"Pay him what's necessary. We'll wait outside."

Ducking their heads, and hurrying to be out of the stench, the two exited through the small door. Moving away from the odor that seemed to follow them like a rolling fog bank, they both took deep, appreciative lung-fulls of fresh air. A moment later Sara joined them. She handed Kirk a much-depleted purse, and shouldered a neelot-skin bag.

"This way," she said, and started diagonally across the market square.

"I hope that's not what I think it is," McCoy said, prodding the bag she carried as they wove their way through the crowd.

"Prime *vris*," Sara said as she turned her nose away from the bag. "Old Vembe's hill code wouldn't let him take a bribe. But he found nothing in it against selling me ten kilos at three times the going rate. At least now, though, we know where Chag Gara lives. It's not too far from here."

She stepped through the narrow spaces between the closely grouped buildings heading back in the direction they had come.

"Anybody in the mood for *vris?*"

Kirk and McCoy stared at her and shook their heads in a vigorous negative.

"Somehow, I thought that's what you gentlemen would say," she grimaced and heaved the bag onto a pile of trash.

Twenty minutes later, after walking down the slope leading to the western sea's bay, they paused near the edge of a marsh. The salty tang in the air from the wind-borne sea spray tingled their nostrils. They breathed it in deeply, flushing out the last remnants of the stench of the *vris*. The bay and the sea were visible beyond the marsh, tinged a deep blue, almost violet, by the rays of Kyr.

Only one kind of vegetation seemed to be growing in the marsh. Barrel-shaped plants with five or six slender, spiky leaves jutting from their tops and jiggling in a gentle land breeze, made a mat that glowed golden-yellow in the sun's rays. Among the plants moved harvesters, who tore off the leaves and piled them on sledges they dragged through the mud behind them.

"*Jakim*," George explained. "Lumber is scarce in Andros, and once those leaves are processed, they can be woven into mats that are almost as strong as steel."

She looked around as if searching for a landmark and then, nodding with satisfaction, stepped off to the right. A few minutes later, she led the way into a narrow, winding street. Soon the smell of *vris* was in the air again. Sara explained that they were in the section of the city inhabited almost solely by exiled hill-men. The street wasn't paved, and an evil-smelling sewer meandered down its center. Sara in the lead, they picked their way down a walkway made of *jakim* mats, stepping over piles of trash and broken crockery. From somewhere in the distance came the sound of angry, drunken voices and a woman's scream.

Only half of the mud-walled, dome-shaped, single dwellings seemed to be inhabited. The sky could be seen through barred windows in some of the homes where the roofs had fallen in. Ragged, emaciated children played on weed-covered plots among the rubble of collapsed walls.

"Poor devils," McCoy muttered softly. "Any system that forces people to live like this should be changed."

"You're right, Bones," Kirk agreed, "but it isn't our place to change it and Spock's way would only make things worse. Planets like Kyros have to be allowed to find their own way in their own time. That's why we have General Order One."

Ensign George paused suddenly and pointed across the street.

"I think this is it," she said. "Vembe told me it would be a small house on the left with a red and black door directly across from a wine shop. This is the wine shop . . ." she gestured to the building behind them. ". . . and that seems to be the only place which fits the description." Turning to Kirk, the ensign asked, "What now?"

Kirk peered at Chag Gara's dwelling for a moment, then said, "From what we know of Gara's proclivities, he'd be more likely to let a woman alone in, rather than one accompanied by a pair of men. If Dr. McCoy gives you the hypo, do you think you can handle Gara? We'll be right outside in case of trouble."

"Trust my dop," Sara said, giving a confident nod. "She can handle any man."

"Bones . . ." Kirk said. McCoy handed Sara the hypo and she slipped it into her chiton. She picked her way across the muddy street, soiling her slippers in the process. When she raised her hand to knock on the red and black striped door, a strange metamorphosis took place. Simply standing before the solid door, she became wanton and provocative.

"Can that be our prim Sara?" Kirk whispered to McCoy. "I think I'd like to meet that dop of hers."

McCoy nodded agreement. Sara knocked, waited, and then knocked again, cocking her head as if listening for movement inside. There was no response.

"Asleep, or out?" Kirk muttered.

She turned and beckoned to them. They picked their way across the street and joined her at the door. Kirk made a gesture for silence, seized a projecting wooden lever, raised it carefully, then in one swift movement, flung open the door.

"Inside!"

They burst into a deserted building.

A rickety table stood in the center of the small, dusty one-room dwelling. On it was a dirty plate, a pottery jug, and an empty wine cup. An old crate beside it served as a chair. The walls were bare except for a frayed and worn hill robe that hung from a peg. To one side, a cot-like bed was overturned and a coarsely woven mattress had tumbled to the floor.

"Too late . . ." Sara murmured.

Kirk gazed around the house saying nothing for a few moments. He walked to the overturned bed and prodded the mattress with one foot. "Spock has him," he said finally. "That's obvious. The only question is . . . where?"

Sighing, he walked to the open door of Gara's hovel. Directly across the street, a small group of hill people arrived at the wine shop. Two women separated themselves from the group and sat to one side of the wide-open entrance. The men went in.

"Maybe . . . maybe someone over there saw what happened and which direction Spock took," Kirk said. "Let's check it out."

"I don't think I can go," Sara said dubiously. "It's taboo for women to drink in hill wine shops. *Vris* is one thing; wine is something else again."

"It's even taboo for women like your dop?" McCoy asked.

Sara nodded. Kirk shrugged. "All they can do is throw us out."

They started across the narrow street, stepping carefully to avoid the worst of the muck, when a sudden hubbub of angry voices came from within the wine shop. A giant of a man in a fiery red mask, followed by an angry hillman waving a piece of slate, came charging out of the wine shop holding a small, roly-poly Kyrosian by the scruff of his neck and the seat of his pants. The large man gave a tremendous heave, and the little man went flying through the air, landing with a soggy splat in the noisome, garbage-laden streamlet in the center of the street.

He sat there a minute as if trying to get his bearings. Slowly, he rose to his feet. He craned his head back, and ruefully surveyed the befouled seat of his baggy shorts. Wrinkling his pudgy nose in distaste, he reached back with one hand as if to wipe off the malodorous mud, then seemed to think better of it. Apparently unable to cope with the situation, he just stood there helplessly, a woebegone expression on his chubby face.

"Say," Ensign George said slowly. "I know I've seen that face before." She thought for a moment. "He's dressed differently; I think he was wearing some kind of robes before—but I could almost swear I snapped his profile the morning I came down. I'd have to check the mag-cards to be sure."

"Let's see if we can't help him with his immediate problem," McCoy said and went into Chag Gara's hovel.

A moment later, he came out with the frayed hill robe and, making a mopping gesture handed it to the little man. He took it gratefully and, after vigorous scrubbing on the seat of his pants and the backs of his fat legs, handed it back to McCoy with a courtly bow and a spatter of guttural Kyrosian.

At Kirk's inquiry, Sara translated. "He says we've earned the gratitude of Ker Kaseme, first among healers."

"Ah," said Kirk, "that explains McCoy's concern. A colleague was in distress."

"Simply a matter of professional courtesy, Jim," McCoy said, tossing the soiled robe through the open door of Chag Gara's hovel.

"Sara," he added, "I must admit to a certain curiosity as to why the 'first among healers' was bounced from a slum bar at ten o'clock in the morning. Ask him —diplomatically, of course."

She shot the little man a quick question. His reply was a rather lengthy one, punctuated by many gesticulations.

"There's an 'ex' in front of his title," Sara said. "It seems that jealous colleagues had him expelled as head of the Healer's Guild on trumped-up charges involving alleged misconduct with certain of his younger female patients. As a result, he is now destitute and forced to have his morning cup . . ."

The little man swayed slightly and hiccuped.

"Better make that 'cups,' " she amended, ". . . at an establishment that is somewhat more modest than it has been his custom to frequent. This morning there was an unfortunate incident, a misunderstanding over a several-day-old bar bill."

Kirk looked at McCoy. "Say, Bones," he said, "we may have something here. As a rule, a barfly doesn't wander far from his home. Sara, ask him if he's noticed anything unusual going on over here." Kirk gestured to Chag Gara's house.

Ker Kaseme started to reply to Sara's question. Suddenly, his voice hoarsened. He croaked out a few more words and then, smiling apologetically, brought an imaginary wine bowl to his lips and made sipping sounds.

"He says that he's had an attack of an old throat condition that makes speech impossible, but that perhaps some wine might relieve the spasm." Sara smiled and shrugged her shoulders as she translated. "Seems our day to get taken," she added.

The little man croaked a few more words and pointed up the street in the direction of the harbor.

"He says he did observe something unusual last night. When his voice recovers, he'd be glad to tell us about it. In the meantime, he recommends a wine shop near here which is patronized by *jakim* weavers. After what was just done to him, he refuses to honor the local establishment with his presence any longer."

"It seems he's got us over a barrel," Kirk said. "Let's go. We've got to find out about Chag Gara!"

The little healer in the lead, they set off through a maze of winding streets and alleys, until at last he halted at the entrance to a wine shop that seemed no more prepossessing than the one across from Chag Gara's. He bowed and waved for the other three to enter.

It was dark inside, and the ceiling was so low that Kirk had to duck to keep from bumping his head on a low-hanging beam. The odor of hot, highly spiced wine filled the place, and animal fat lamps along the walls cast deep shadows across the scattered tables. A sprinkling of customers, already well into their drinking day in spite of the earliness of the hour, sat hunched, staring intently into their wine bowls as if waiting for some important message or revelation.

The rotund man tossed his gray locks and led Kirk and the rest to a long, high table at the back, which served as a bar, and pounded his fist on its top in thirsty impatience.

A hulking Kyrosian behind the table was ladling wine from a steaming cauldron into a bowl held in the shaking hands of an obviously hung-over customer. He turned his head in Kaseme's direction.

As soon as he saw who was there, he laid the ladle down carefully. Then, moving swiftly and smiling malevolently, he advanced on Kaseme, growling in Kyrosian. Kaseme let out a squeak of terror and scuttled behind Kirk's broad back for protection.

The tavern owner's little red pig eyes fastened on Kirk.

"What now, Sara?" Kirk demanded, staring back at the wine shop operator.

After a rapid exchange, Sara reported. "Kaseme has a bar bill problem here, too. The bartender says he'll take it out of Kaseme's hide, if he isn't paid now."

Kirk tossed the money pouch to Sara. "Find out what it is and pay it," he said impatiently. "We haven't got all day."

At a quick word from Sara, the bartender's scowl vanished. He turned to a shelf stacked high with smooth, black slates, rummaged through them, finally producing one almost completely covered with hatch marks. It took nearly all of Kirk's remaining money to wipe it clean.

Kaseme, no longer feeling endangered, snapped an order in a haughty voice and led the party to a table. He went through his first jug of wine in no time at all, and was waving for a refill when Kirk caught his wrist, calling a halt.

"Tell him that's all the medicine he gets until I get some answers," he ordered.

Kaseme looked woebegone at Sara's words, croaking and rubbing his throat. Kirk glared at him. Kaseme shot a wistful glance at his jug, then began to talk. When he was finished, Sara snapped a few more questions. He responded to each with a shrug and a raising of his palms indicating he didn't know the answers. Finally, in response to a question from Kaseme, Sara nodded her head. The little man took his wine jug and trotted happily to the bar.

"Well?" Kirk said.

"Problems," she said unhappily. "Less than an hour ago, a tall hillman wearing a black and red clan mask went into Chag Gara's house. When he came out, he was carrying a figure wrapped in a blanket over one shoulder. Ker said a couple of the neighbors tried to interfere, but the hooded man paralyzed them with just a touch. So they let him carry Chag Gara away."

"The nerve pinch!" McCoy burst out.

"Yes," Kirk said nodding somberly. "It has to be Spock. Only a Vulcan can do that, and now he's got Gara."

"It looks as if Spock is invulnerable now," McCoy muttered.

"We'll find a way to stop him," Kirk replied, his voice ringing with more confidence than perhaps he actually felt. Kaseme returned from the bar and plopped down happily, sipped from his wine bowl, and watched the other three talk.

"There's nothing we can do down here now," Kirk said. "We'd better get up to the ship and figure out our next move." He began to stand, but McCoy, gazing at the smiling, curious face of Ker Kaseme, held up a hand.

"Just a second, Jim. We may be missing a bet here."

"Specify."

"Our friend here." McCoy tipped his head toward the healer. "Dops are fine as far as they go, but we're still strangers in town."

"So?" Kirk demanded. "What does Kaseme have to do with it?"

"He knows the town. As a healer, he had to have

been able to move through all the levels of society. He may be down at the heels now, but he was head of the guild. He probably has a lot of important, official friends who might help us. And," McCoy looked around at the somnolent figures slumped at the tables of the dingy bar, "he certainly knows the seamier side of Andros rather intimately, I imagine. I think it's about time we put Scotty to work on our secret weapon."

"What do you mean?" Sara asked curiously.

"Money." McCoy tapped Kirk's depleted purse which lay on the table. "Scotty can turn out perfect replicas of the local coinage for us by the bushel, using the matter converters. I'll bet if we filled Kaseme's pockets full enough, he could get the charges against him dropped in no time. He'd make a perfect front man."

Kirk nodded thoughtfully. "You're right, Bones. We can't use the inn as our safe house any longer. Spock knows about it, and he's apt to counterattack any time. If Ker could get back into the Healer's Guild, he could rent a house as a clinic. It would be a perfect cover for our operations."

The little Kyrosian drained his bowl and smiled at Kirk. Kirk smiled back and handed him the purse of coins.

"Sara, ask him if . . ."

CHAPTER SEVEN

Captain's log: Stardate 6724.2:
Ker Kaseme is once again a healer in good standing.
He is so delighted with his sudden change of fortune
that he has his proclivity toward wine and women under
control and is giving us absolute cooperation. He has
opened a clinic in a large house near the central square.
The back of it is reserved for our use and, because of the
constant flow of patients in and out of the clinic part,
we can enter and leave without question. McCoy and I
now have implants and we are able to pass as native
healers, members of Kaseme's staff. Kaseme knows
which side his bread is buttered on and has accepted our
identity switch. He must be puzzled, though, when Mc-
Coy displays some of his own mannerisms. Kaseme
doesn't know it, of course, but he is our chief surgeon's
dop.
Kaseme's contacts have reported the location of
Spock's headquarters. Unfortunately, it is so well
guarded by his hill followers that any direct assault is
out of the question. We have been unable to come up
with a plan for forcible entry that wouldn't alert Spock
in time for him to carry out his threat to destroy the
trilithium modules.
Spock is up to something—a number of hill chiefs
have visited him in the last two days—but we haven't
been able to find out what it is. Little time is left. Un-
less we can recover the crystals in the next five days, we
will be forced to abandon the Enterprise.

Captain James Kirk, now known as Healer Hirga,
sat at a makeshift desk in a room at the rear of
Kaseme's clinic. Dr. McCoy, alias Healer Makai, snored
softly on a cot at the far side of the room. Behind Kirk,

a heavy door closed off the room used as a transporter terminal. Since communicators couldn't be used to call the *Enterprise* for a pick-up because of the Messiah's threat, a schedule had been worked out that automatically energized the transporters every fifteen minutes. Time was measured by a large and complicated water clock that stood beside Kirk's desk.

Kirk rose to his feet as a faint hum sounded from the inner room. A moment later the door opened and Lieutenant Commander Scott entered the room.

"I think this will do the job, Captain," he said, handing Kirk a silver rod which was richly ornamented with gold rings and jeweled studs.

Kirk turned the rod over in his hands and examined it critically. "Good job, Scotty," he said. "It'll pass as a healer's wand—same heft and everything. How does it work?"

"If I may, sir," Scott said, taking the wand back. He pointed to one stud set with a tiny opal. "The trigger. The band next to it is the safety. Turn it to the right to activate the firing mechanism. Like this." He turned the ring and pointed it toward the cot where McCoy lay sleeping. When he pressed the stud there was a slight hiss and then a *thunk* as a tiny dart slammed into the wall a few centimeters above McCoy's head. The sleeping doctor woke with a start.

"What was that?" he said in a blurry voice.

"Naething," Scott said. "Go back to sleep." He handed the wand back to Kirk. "There's a clip o' twenty darts in the butt. Each one is made from 1.4 hyperpyroxine which will dissolve instantly upon impact. Paralysis is instantaneous, according to Dr. Mbenga. Anybody hit with one of those won't be able to move a muscle for at least an hour. The range is limited though, aboot ten meters. You'll have to get pretty close to Mr. Spock to hit him."

"No problem there," Kirk said. "Healers are privileged people on Kyros, and after Spock is down, his bodyguards won't want to bother us." He glanced at the water clock. "Only a few hours left. Is the landing party standing by?"

"Aye, sir," Scott replied. "The twenty with implants are disguised as hillmen and will meet you in the square. I'll have another twenty armed with Kyrosian weapons here as a back-up force in case of trouble."

"Good," Kirk said. "When you get back up to the ship, notify Security Chief Pulaski that there's been a slight change of plans. Ker brought me word an hour ago that the time of Spock's mass meeting has been moved up from early dusk to late dusk. I don't know why, but Spock never does anything without a reason. There's been a whispering campaign going on about the powers of the new Messiah. He's promised to perform a spectacular public miracle tonight. I imagine half the town will be there."

"The more, the better," McCoy said, rising from the bunk. "There'll be just that much more confusion when Kaseme's boys go into action."

"I thought you were asleep," Kirk said.

"With you shooting things at me . . . ?" McCoy replied.

There was a soft tap on the closed outer door. "It's Ker Kaseme, honored friends," a voice called. "May I enter?"

"In a moment," Kirk said. "Scotty," he said in a low voice, "get into the other room. Ker is doing a fine job of keeping his eyes closed to our comings and goings, but an officer in Fleet uniform might be too much." He glanced at the water clock. "The next beam-up is due in a few minutes, anyway."

Scott nodded and went into the back room. Kirk followed him to the door. "McCoy and I will be out with Kaseme for the next couple of hours getting things organized for this evening. Bring the landing party down around 17:30. You stand by with your men here. Once the other group is in position in the plaza, Ensign George will notify me. McCoy and I will be in front of Vembe's."

"Aye, sir," Scott acknowledged the orders. "An' I hope that little widget does the trick."

"You haven't let me down yet, Scotty," Kirk said as he closed and barred the door. He crossed the room and opened the outer door. "Enter, honored friend," he said, shifting effortlessly into Kyrosian. Kaseme entered and bobbed a greeting.

"Have you gotten enough men?" Kirk asked.

"Yes, but it wasn't as easy as I thought it would be," Kaseme replied. "I had to pay three times as much as I expected and promise to pay twice as much when the fracas is over." He pulled out an almost empty purse and eyed it ruefully.

"There's a lot more where that came from," Kirk said. "Why was it hard to get the men?"

"The Messiah," Kaseme answered. "Until he showed up, our city slum types, miserable as they were, had one thing going for them. Bad as their lot was, there was always one group they could look down on, the hill outcasts who had drifted into Andros because they had no place else to go. They're the ones who have always done the dirty jobs no one else would touch, but now they're walking tall. They're carrying arms and no longer step into the gutter when they meet an Androsian on a narrow sidewalk. My *zreels* aren't too happy about picking on someone who might fight back."

"What about the provost guard?" Kirk asked.

"That's taken care of. I didn't have to bribe the watch commander much to gain his cooperation. There's no room for him and his men in the Messiah's 'New Order,' and they're itching for an excuse to bash in a few hill skulls. Once trouble starts, they'll be in there swinging. But they've been ordered to stay away from the immediate vicinity of the Messiah, so they shouldn't interfere with your plans."

"Good," Kirk said. "Where are your men?"

"I've got them spotted in little groups in taverns all over town. I didn't dare assemble them in one place; there are too many of the Messiah's agents around. I've left orders, though, that their wine be doled out in scanty rations so they're not too drunk to be of use." Kaseme fell silent.

Kirk rose to his feet. "All right. It'll take us several hours to make the rounds with final instructions, so let's suit up, Bones, and get going."

He took two hooded white robes, with crimson slashes across their fronts, from pegs on the wall and tossed one to McCoy. After he'd slipped his on, he adjusted its folds carefully. As he picked up his silver wand from the table, he saw Kaseme gaze at it with obvious envy. Kaseme's own carved wooden one looked cheap and gaudy by comparison.

"If our healing goes off on schedule," Kirk said, "you can have this one. Call it a gift from a grateful patient."

He glanced at McCoy who nodded his readiness.

"Let's go."

Captain Kirk drew his white healer's robe tighter about him and shivered as a chill wind blew across the plaza. He had his hood pulled up, and his features were almost indistinguishable in the darkness.

"Looks like a storm blowing up," McCoy remarked.

"I'm not surprised," Kirk said. "That radiation front is beginning to interfere with the planetary weather patterns, in spite of an ozone layer twice Earth's standard."

He peered out at the plaza. "It doesn't seem to have affected the turnout, though."

"Curiosity seems to be a trait basic to most intelligent life," McCoy remarked.

The two stood in silence for a moment, looking out from their vantage point under the arcade archway in front of Vembe's shop. Its doors were closed and, happily, only a faint scent of *vris* lingered to pollute the air.

As they watched, the crowd in the square grew denser.

"It looks like Kaseme's men are starting to arrive," Kirk muttered, as roughly dressed men in groups of twos and threes, some lurching slightly, emerged from side streets and began to infiltrate the growing throng.

Thunder growled overhead, and a faint flicker of light glimmered briefly in the sky.

"Captain!" A whisper came from behind them. Kirk turned, and a scantily dressed figure stepped out of the gloom. It was Ensign George.

"Aren't you freezing in that outfit?" McCoy asked solicitously.

"I sure am," she replied, "but it would be out of character if I didn't display the merchandise."

"Is everything set?" Kirk asked.

Sara nodded. "Commander Pulaski is standing by for final instructions." She gestured toward a cluster of men in hill dress standing on the other side of the square.

"Tell them," Kirk began, "that as soon as Spock arrives, they are to get as close to him as possible. When Kaseme's men start the riot, I want them to form a flying wedge and be ready to open a path through the crowd and out of there. I'm banking on there being so much confusion that Spock's bodyguards won't question our actions."

"I'll tell Pulaski," Sara said, and headed across the square, attracting admiring glances and occasional shouted compliments as she undulated through the crowd.

A flash of lighting suddenly illuminated the square, and a stiff blast of wind almost extinguished the recently lighted oil lamps set on pillars along the arcade. A moment later a rumble of thunder sounded from the direction of the distant moutains. Kirk glanced worriedly at the sky. Tattered streamers of clouds, pale and ghostlike, skittered across the northern sky. An occasional early star gleamed between the rents in the clouds, and on the western horizon only a lurid red glow marked the place where Kyr had set.

"Look, Bones," Kirk muttered. The doctor craned his head upward. Flickering, shifting, but ever growing, a dancing veil of light was forming, snaking between the racing clouds.

"An aurora," Kirk went on. "I wonder if that's Spock's promised miracle."

"I doubt it," McCoy said, shaking his head. "My dop remembers seeing one when he was a child, so auroras aren't unusual even this far south."

"Well, whatever this 'miracle' is, I hope the weather holds off," Kirk said. "Most of the crowd is here for a free show, and a heavy rain would send them scuttling for cover."

Twilight deepened. The wind died to small, unpredictable gusts that seemed to be coming from every direction. The sky overhead cleared and most of the cloud cover seemed to be concentrated on the horizon. Suddenly, there was a rumble of hill drums and the sound of distant chanting came from a narrow street that opened onto the square.

Then the sound grew louder, as the high-pitched, strangely atonal skirling of native pipes fluted above the deep bass of the drums. A hush fell over the square, as thirty or forty clansmen mounted on hissing neelots began to open a path through the crowd.

There was a final pipe and drum crescendo as the procession entered the square, and then a sudden, dramatic silence. A hollow square of torch-bearing hillmen appeared; an alien army whose sinister masks, fitfully illuminated by the flaring, dancing torchlight, made them appear like a host from hell. In their center, drawn by four matched black neelots, was a windowless, hearse-like vehicle painted jet black.

As the procession neared the center of the square, Kirk, McCoy at his heels, headed rapidly toward it. Hillmen ringed the van, holding back the curious crowd that pressed in.

As the two *Enterprise* officers pushed their way through the throng, hooded hillmen and gally dressed city folk alike stepped aside deferentially at the sight of their white healers' robes. Just as they reached the front ranks of the circle of spectators, there was a roll of drums. A trapdoor opened on the roof of the van, just behind the driver's seat, and a black-robed figure appeared. He stood for a moment, head bowed as if in deep thought. His waist was circled by a wide leather belt. A mace-like weapon swung at his right hip; attached to his left was a small, rectangular black box. As the Messiah turned, scanning the crowd from behind his red and black hood, Kirk gazed fixedly at the box.

"Bones, look," he whispered. "Spock has the tricorder on him." Kirk raised his eyes to the figure's face. He felt safe from detection behind his healer's robe, but a glance from the Messiah made him turn away. As he did so, a soft sigh escaped his lips. "Spock . . ."

The Messiah slowly raised both arms to the sky as if in supplication. As he lowered them, he spread them wide as though to embrace the crowd. Tall in the torchlight, he began to speak. His voice was low, almost inaudible, and a silence held the crowd as they strained to hear what he had to say.

At first, in spite of the drama of the torchlight and the hooded followers, he sounded like any other street preacher inveighing against a long catalog of acts which the gods considered sinful, coming down especially hard on pleasures of the body. The crowd began to stir restlessly.

"What's he doing?" Kirk muttered. "Another couple of minutes of this and people will start to go home."

"I think he's pulling an old debater's trick," McCoy answered softly. "Once he's got them completely off guard, he's going to let them have it."

His prediction was right. Suddenly, the Messiah's voice took on a ringing timbre and boomed through the square as if amplified.

"You tire of the old words? Good, they've kept you divided and confused for too long. Tonight, I bring the new—new words for a new day—" He paused dramatically. "And a sign to seal them by. Listen, my children, the gods have no quarrel with the pleasures of the flesh—love, food, and drink are their gifts to lighten your days. But on Kyros there is little love, and the poor go hungry. And wine is used to deaden misery rather than as a source of joy.

"Why should such things be in a world the gods created for your delight? In your hearts you know the answer. Look to your masters, the oppressive few who feed on your distress and rob you of your birthright from the gods. Our world is splintered into tiny states, each ruled by little groups of greedy men, bloated parasites whose taloned hands wield taxes, police, and jails!

"But the gods have eyes! The gods have ears! And now, their wrath—too long withheld—descends! For behold, I have been ordained and sent among you to lead you to the light, a messiah for the golden age to come.

Through me, all Kyros will be united into one people: one people believing as one, thinking as one, worshipping as one. You shall be my body and I shall be your soul; you, my sword, and I, your shield. And through me you shall find such glory and blessings as you have never known in all your troubled days."

As he spoke, the Messiah's arms and extended hands beat up and down, punctuating the rhythmic flow of his words. Shadows cast by the flaming torches surrounding him danced on the buildings facing the plaza.

A low rumble of thunder sounded from the darkening sky as the speaker chanted his vision of the days that were to come, a vision of Kyros united, where there were no longer slaves and masters, no longer rich and poor, no longer hunger and suffering and oppression. Then a note of menace entered his voice as he shifted from the future to the present. There were those, he rumbled, who would attempt to thwart the will of the gods, parasites who would never willingly surrender their power. For those, he pledged, there would be no mercy.

His voice rose higher and higher until it was at once shrill and nearly hysterical and yet, at the same time, as commanding and booming as the distant, growling thunder.

Kirk had a sudden memory of an ancient history tape of a small, moustached man wearing an armband with a twisted cross on it, molding a vast amphitheater of people into a single, screaming beast with the magic of his voice. The Messiah's arms pumped and suddenly stopped. Kirk heard a faint buzz come from the box on the figure's hip. The Messiah flung his arms up and pointed to the eastern horizon. That area of the sky was still clear of clouds, and a few stars shone through a dancing, shifting veil of rainbow colors that was draped across a full sixty degrees in a rippling aurora. But that didn't cause the sudden gasp of fearful awe.

One star was moving!

CHAPTER EIGHT

"Behold . . . Afterbliss!"

The Messiah's cry rang through the square and the eyes of the crowd followed the pointing arm of the black-robed man. The new star rose, a shimmering pearl of white that climbed swiftly up the vault of the heavens, moving across the sky toward Andros.

"Behold the work of the gods, a dwelling place of everlasting delight for those who follow their will and their chosen Messiah. Death in battle is no longer death, but a gateway to eternal life. The swords of the ungodly may pierce our bodies and spill our blood on the dry ground, but with each rising of our heavenly home, the gods shall lift our dead to their reward. And for those who resist the divine will"—the Messiah's voice growled his message of warning again—"another place has been prepared, a place of burning and eternal torment!"

As the new star moved on its downward course, dropping to the western horizon, the torch-bearing hillmen who ringed the wagon began a barking chant, continuing through the minutes the star was visible.

"Death! Death to unbelievers! Death to the Messiah's enemies!"

Scattered voices in the crowd began to pick it up, and the Messiah himself joined in, cracking out the staccato words.

"Death! Death! Death!"

Raw, demonic power seemed to pour from the black-robed man, and more and more voices from the crowd began to join in. Feet began to stomp on the paving stones of the plaza, a thrumming, echoing sound. Shoulders began to sway.

Kirk found himself caught up in tidal currents of building emotion that threatened to swirl him out of control. Bit by bit, his will began to ebb, surrendering to that hammering, hypnotic voice.

He dug his nails into his palms, hoping to use pain as a defense against the web of madness being woven by the Messiah's siren call. The urge to join, to become one with the chanting, howling crowd, mounted to irresistibility.

He fought for control of his body as it tried to stamp and jerk in cadence with the rest of the puppets, whose movements were orchestrated by the wildly waving arms of the black-robed magician. In spite of the chill of the evening, sweat dripped from Kirk's contorted face. His healer's wand slipped unnoticed from writhing fingers and fell to the ground.

"Jim!" a voice called, seemingly from a great distance. A hand gripped his forearm in a vise-like grasp. He tried to shake it off, but it only clamped down harder. Kirk grunted in pain, pain which broke through the oratory-induced trance.

"Jim! Snap out of it. Spock's miracle—that was the *Enterprise!* It had to be."

Kirk gave a dazed shake of his head, trying to cast off the grip of the emotional spell projected by the chanting figure on the roof of the wagon.

"Somehow he's forced Sulu to change orbit; she can't be more than a hundred and fifty kilometers up," McCoy hissed into his ear. "Get the wand; you've got to stop that madman before it's too late. Another few minutes of this, and he'll have everyone under his control."

Sudden anger blossomed in Kirk, clearing his head. His ship, a pawn in the Messiah's mad game! Aware that he had dropped the wand, Kirk bent and snatched it up. With shaking hands, he pointed it toward the capering figure on the van and pressed the firing stud.

"Death! Death to un—"

In mid-word, the Messiah slapped his hands to his chest, staggered a step, then pitched over the edge of the van like a giant, broken-winged crow.

A shocked gasp rose from the crowd. Hillmen

dropped their torches and leaped to his rescue. Their reaching arms caught him, lowering the Messiah gently to the ground.

With the snapping of the hypnotic spell that had held them in thrall, voices of protest began to rise here and there as the personal implications of the Messiah's revolutionary pronouncement began to sink in. Somewhat belatedly, Kaseme's men remembered why they were there and broke out in a chorus of hooting jeers. The Messiah's followers began to shout back.

Shoving began, and in moments the square was filled with cursing, struggling knots of Kyrosians, some trying to escape, others plunging into the melee.

"Come on, Bones," Kirk muttered. The two officers began to shove their way into the seething mass, heading for the black van. Units of the provost guard came trotting out of several side streets in disciplined formations. The squads broke up, and the guards, truncheons swinging, charged into the mob.

Hillmen milled in the center of the square, clustering defensively around their fallen leader.

"Make way," Kirk shouted authoritatively. "Make way so we may help the Messiah!"

The two burst upon the ring of hillmen and met only snarls of distrust. Dirks and swords, hidden under robes until then, gleamed wickedly in the torchlight.

"Put down those weapons," Kirk snapped. "We're here to help him, not to harm him."

The clansmen glanced at each other in a moment of indecision. Finally, at a guttural command from a hillman who knelt by the Messiah's head, the blades were lowered. Kirk moved forward, knelt by the Messiah, and placed his ear against the robe-covered chest.

In a voice easily heard by those who clustered around, McCoy asked, "Is he dead?"

Kirk glanced up and shook his head. "Not yet, but he will be soon unless we get him to a place of healing." He rose to his feet.

"Your Messiah is dying. We cannot help him here. He must be taken to our clinic at once."

The other stared at him, and also rose to his feet.

"No," he said obdurately, "we will take him to the hills. The gods will not let him die."

"Who are you to know their will?" Kirk snapped. "His breath is failing. In minutes he'll be dead."

He scanned the hooded figures who pressed close around until he spotted a couple of quick head nods that identified *Enterprise* crewmen in hill disguise. He beckoned to them.

"You and you. Pick up your master. Gently, now."

Kirk led them to the rear of the van, unlatched the doors, and swung them open.

"Inside," he said, his voice commanding. "There's no time to lose."

As the Messiah was laid gently on the floor of the wagon, a little whimpering sound came from its dark interior. Kirk peered into the darkness and could vaguely make out a hooded figure curled on a blanket in a foetal position.

"Bones, it's Chag Gara," he whispered to the doctor. "We've got them both. Let's get them out of here fast."

The two officers jumped out of the wagon, and Kirk slammed the doors shut. He and McCoy went quickly around the side of the black van and clambered into the front seat.

"Hillmen!" Kirk shouted. "Open a way through the crowd. Hurry!"

There was a quick stir as disguised crew members formed a wedge in front of the van. They pushed forward and through the screaming, rioting crowd.

Kirk grabbed the reins and flapped them to get the neelots into motion. As the van lumbered forward, torch-bearing hillmen trotted along its flanks, knives and swords exposed again, ready to defend their leader. From his high vantage point, Kirk could see that his plan was working well.

Some of Kaseme's men were joyfully smashing rock-like fists into the faces of some of the hillmen scattered through the crowd. Others of the half-drunken irregulars fought fiercely with clubs and swords, while still more seized opportunity and paused occasionally to lift the purses of unconscious townspeople.

The provost guards added to the confusion as they milled through the crowd, clubbing to the ground any masked figure they came upon.

"Looks like we made it, Bones," Kirk muttered, as the van emerged from the seething ocean of chaos in the plaza into the relative quiet of the narrow lane that led to the clinic's compound. It lay to the left, in the middle of the lane, and as they approached it, the doors of the courtyard gate began to swing open.

"Chalk one up for our side," Kirk said. "In a couple of hours, Spock will be back to normal, and the *Enterprise* will be warping out of here."

The advance guard of the disguised *Enterprise* men turned as it reached the now open gate. As Kirk pulled back on the reins to slow down the neelots, there was a creaking noise behind them and McCoy twisted in his seat, glancing back.

"Jim!" he shouted. "Watch out! It's—"

His voice ended in a gasp as a black-robed arm shot out and, wielding a club, clipped McCoy on the temple. He slumped forward, unconscious.

Kirk spun around, fumbling to get his wand in position to fire a dart into the black-robed figure who had just emerged from the trapdoor in the roof of the van. The Messiah's club swung toward Kirk, but he dodged like a cat, arcing his arm around, aiming at his snarling antagonist.

He fired . . . and missed. A sudden, slashing blow of the figure's club smashed into his right shoulder with brutal force. The wand dropped from suddenly nerveless fingers.

Surrounded by a haze of blinding red pain, Kirk fumbled with his left hand on the floor of the driver's box to recover the wand. Before he could locate it, powerful arms gripped him tightly and lifted him high.

He felt himself hurled to the cobbled street below.

He lay half stunned for a moment, struggling to regain his breath and balance. He rolled weakly onto all fours as a stentorian voice rumbled above him.

"Demons!" the voice shouted. "Demons in disguise who seek my life. Kill them!"

His useless arm dangling at his side, Kirk staggered to his feet and looked wildly up at the shouting figure giving orders to his hooded followers in the street.

"The drug . . ." Kirk muttered half to himself as he stumbled toward the van, ". . . he threw it off. Bones . . ."

As screaming hillmen, their blades making a deadly fence, crowded close to the van to defend their Messiah, Kirk lurched toward it, a haze of pain filming his vision.

He slipped through the ranks of the fighting hillmen and, reaching up with his good arm, grabbed the unconscious doctor by one foot. As he tried to drag the surgeon to safety, the van gave a sudden lurch forward. The frightened neelots screamed and reared, sparks and chips of stone flying from their hammering hooves.

Kirk was tossed backward. His head slammed against the van, and blinding explosions of pain ripped through his skull. He collapsed onto his knees.

He struggled to rise, but fell sprawling onto his back. Paralyzed by pain, he blinked up helplessly at the hooded hillmen who closed in like vultures.

Then the tide of red crested, leaving blackness in its wake.

CHAPTER NINE

When Kirk finally came to, he found himself being half-carried, half-dragged somewhere. As he struggled feebly to escape, a familiar Scot's burr murmured over him.

"Easy does it, Captain, we'll hae you safe in a minute."

"McCoy," Kirk mumbled, "get McCoy, Scotty . . ."

"He's safe, sir," Scott replied. "Some of the boys grabbed him just after you fell. We came charging out when Spock popped up like a jack-in-the-box and put you and Dr. McCoy out of commission."

Kirk felt himself lowered gently to the ground on his back. He sat up with difficulty, and his head swam. He realized he was well inside the courtyard. Several *Enterprise* wounded lay near.

Scott shouted orders to a handful of men and they rushed back to the fighting going on at the gate. As the rear-guard action went on, and the gate slowly closed, Kirk saw the van, a black-robed figure in the driver's seat, slowly work its way out of the mass of fighting men and disappear down the street. The night echoed with the cries of enraged, vengeful clansmen.

Kirk rose shakily to his feet, glanced down at the unconscious body of McCoy, and then staggered over to help close the gate. He picked up a heavy bludgeon someone had dropped and lurched into the fray.

As a hill sword slashed toward him, he swung an awkward, but powerful, left-handed blow. There was a scream, and the audible crunch of shattering bones. The weapon clanged to the stones.

Outnumbered though they were, the *Enterprise* crew slowly pushed the attackers out through the gateway. The wind whipped harder, flinging dust and bits of gravel

along the street, stinging the faces and blinding the eyes
of the unhooded combatants. Thunder rumbled and
slammed through the aurora-painted sky with greater
and greater frequency. Jagged, actinic flashes of light-
ning illuminated the desperate struggle, flash-freezing
the shouting mass of weirdly dressed, sword-wielding
fighters into stroboscopic scenes out of Dante's *Inferno*.

As the disciplined *Enterprise* forces pushed the last
of the attackers into the narrow street, one of the double
gates was forced shut. The other was closed to the point
where only a narrow gap remained. One by one, the defenders slipped into the safety of the courtyard while
those still in the street closed their ranks into an ever-
tightening defensive semicircle.

Kirk ducked as a thrown dirk flashed toward his
head, to bury its needle-like blade in the hard wood of
the gate. Desperately calling on failing strength, he
smashed right and left with his heavy club in such a
berserk rage that the foremost of his attackers flinched
back.

"Inside!" he shouted, and as the last of the defend-
ing party backed through the three-foot gap into the
courtyard, he hurled his club into the face of one at-
tacker. Another, wearing a tiger-striped hood, dove forward in a low tackle to bring him to the ground. Kirk
reached back over his shoulder, grabbed the dirk stuck
in the gate, tore it loose, and knocked the clansman
senseless with the hilt.

As the hillman slumped at Kirk's feet, he skipped
backward to safety and stood, shoulders slumped and
gasping for breath, as the second gate was forced shut
and a stout cross-bar slammed home.

Still half-dazed, Kirk glanced around the courtyard.
Many *Enterprise* wounded lay groaning on the ground
and others were slumped against the courtyard wall.

"Get those people inside," Kirk ordered. "Those
gates won't hold if they decide to ram. Where's Commander Scott?"

"Here, Captain," Scott called, stepping up to Kirk's
side.

"How long until the next beam-up?"

"No idea, sir. My lads and I hae lost all track of time."

At that moment McCoy tottered over, a bloody rag tied around his head. "Let me check you over, Jim," he said. "You look as if a herd of elephants ran over you."

"I'm all right, Bones," the captain replied, massaging his bruised arm gingerly. "At least my right arm is back in order. Take care of the others. Some look pretty bad."

He winced as Lieutenant Dawson was carried past, the hilt of a highly decorated hill knife protruding from between his ribs.

"I'll do what I can," McCoy said. "But without a medikit, I don't know . . ."

Slowly the courtyard was cleared of the injured. The last to be helped through the narrow door at the rear of the compound was a slight, scantily dressed female who had both hands pressing a blood-soaked cloth to her middle.

"Sara . . ." Kirk said, "what were you doing in that mess?"

Her wan face wrinkled in pain as she answered. "I came back here to alert Scotty as soon as the riot began. I tried . . . to help out at the gate . . . I should have practiced swordsmanship longer with Chekov." In a tone of grim satisfaction, she added, "At least . . . I got three of them before . . . they got me."

Her eyelids fluttered and she passed out. Kirk caught her, waved over two officers with a makeshift stretcher, and ordered them into the building. A sudden, resounding boom from the gate spun Kirk around. The doors jounced again as the hillmen rammed them with long heavy poles.

Kirk ran his gaze along the top of the six-meter-high wall, but saw no sign of scaling ladders . . . yet.

As the last of the landing party passed him, he entered a short, narrow corridor and closed the courtyard entrance behind him. Gloomily, he surveyed the flimsy panels and the single, small latch which held the door shut. Another boom sounded outside.

He turned decisively, walked down the corridor, and pushed his way into the crowded room that had been his office. His engineering officer stood beside the water clock watching it with an anxious expression.

" . . . much longer?" McCoy was asking Scott.

"I canna tell from this contraption, Doctor. You'd better get the worst of the wounded into the terminal room so they can be beamed up when they do energize."

"Well, it better be soon or some will . . ." He cut off as Kirk approached.

"Status report," Kirk ordered to McCoy.

"Only a few are really serious—Sara, Dawson, two or three others. I'm afraid to remove that dirk Dawson has in him without a repressor field; he'd hemorrhage to death in a few minutes. Sara's in shock from loss of blood and I don't have any plasma." He shook his head admiringly. "You know, Jim, she may have gotten us into this mess, but when you were in trouble and went down out there, she charged in like a wildcat. Three of those uglies were ready to make mincemeat out of you, but Sara took care of them all. The last one got under her guard, though, and ripped her open."

Kirk clenched his fists as self-recrimination washed through him, and he mentally reviewed the shambles that had been made of a perfect plan.

"If I'd given Spock another shot . . . just to make sure," he murmured. "If we could only use a communicator . . . ifs . . . ifs."

McCoy made a soft sound. "Take it easy, Jim. We tried . . ."

A sudden shout went up from those standing near the transporter terminal. "First group is up!"

"Bones, get Sara and the others in there quick," Kirk snapped. "You, too. Get up to the ship and get to work."

As McCoy hurried off, Kirk turned to Scott. "Scotty, get some men, take that desk, and barricade the outer door. It might buy us some time."

Scott and a few men maneuvered the desk through the crowd of weary defenders and, when they moved aside to let it pass, Kirk caught sight of a small, plump figure huddled in one corner slurping from a wine bottle. Two empty jugs lay beside him.

"Kaseme! Get in there with the rest," Kirk said, pointing to the terminal room.

"What does it matter where I die?" the little man murmured in a slurred voice. "A sword will hurt as much in there as it will here."

A sudden shouting came from the corridor, and Scott and his men burst back into the room. "They've broken through the gates! They'll be here in seconds!"

Scott hurried to Kirk. "We didn't have time to brace the desk right. They'll be through that door in no time at all."

Barely had Scott spoken when a crash resounded in the corridor, and the passage was filled with the wild ululation of hill war cries.

"Everybody in there!" Kirk shouted above the bellowing curses of the clansmen. The *Enterprise* personnel moved quickly into the terminal. Kirk slammed the door leading into the hall, turned, pulled Kaseme to his feet and shoved him into the other room. Kaseme slumped in a corner and drained the rest of his flask.

Kirk pulled the terminal room's door shut seconds before the clansmen burst into the outer room. They began to hammer at the last door between them and their prey.

The door began to splinter as a deep hum filled the room. The top quarter of the door flew inward, narrowly missing Kirk's face, and the crackling, glittering carrier wave of the transporter beam surrounded the party.

"At last," Kirk muttered. The room faded, wavered, then reappeared.

"That damn radiation front is still screwing up the planet's magnetic field," Scott growled.

Kirk jumped to one side as the enraged, hate-twisted face of one of the Messiah's town followers appeared in the gap of the door. The Kyrosian's sword lunged for Kirk's chest. Kirk grabbed a sword from a nearby officer and chopped downward. The townman screamed in agony as his severed hand, still gripping his sword, dropped to the floor. He fell backward, causing a pause in the hillmen's activity.

Weapons ready, Kirk and the others formed a defensive line and waited for the final attack.

At that moment the *Enterprise* reclaimed her own.

Ker Kaseme let out a terrified squeal as the gray walls of the cargo transporter room materialized around him. His face ashen, he clutched Kirk's arm and began to jabber incoherently. Kirk shook him off.

"Later," he growled in Kyrosian. Kaseme gobbled in terror, then fainted. Kirk caught him and lowered him to the deck. McCoy, who was waiting for Kirk, took the little man.

"Status report," Kirk said, his voice showing deep concern for his wounded officers.

"They're in surgery now," McCoy replied. "Mbenga's hands could bring a statue to life. I waited here for you, to let you know."

Kirk nodded his thanks. McCoy went on. "I'll take Kaseme to sickbay and load him with sedatives. He won't remember a thing."

Scott came up to Kirk. "The poor divil. We've scared the living daylights out of him."

Kirk grinned for the first time that day, and said, "I'll bet those hillmen took off like scalded cats when we beamed up right before their eyes."

"Well," Scott said, "if Mr. Spock can arrange a miracle for his people, I guess we can, too."

Kirk's grin flicked off as he stepped toward the transporter console and stabbed the button on the communicator panel.

"Bridge, this is the captain. What the hell was the idea of changing orbit?"

CHAPTER TEN

Captain's log: Stardate 6725.1:
Investigating the orbit change, I have learned that Mr. Spock told Lieutenant Sulu to follow his orders or he'd destroy the trilithium crystals at once.
I cannot fault Sulu for his action; we still have three and one-half days left in which to retrieve the crystals.
After that, it won't matter any more.

Kirk stood at the side of one of the diagnostic beds in the sickbay, looking down at Lieutenant Dawson's sleeping form. He glanced at the indicators on the Feinberg panels above. He nodded in satisfaction as, one-by-one, he checked the readouts.

"He looks a hell of a lot better than I expected him to," he said.

"We got him here just in time," said McCoy. "He'll be back on his feet in a few days."

"And Sara?"

"Almost as good as new," said a weak voice from the other side of the sickbay. Kirk turned and went quickly over to another bed on the other side of the room.

Ensign George, face pale but eyes alert, gave him a wan smile. "They didn't really damage the plumbing," she said. "And Dr. Mbenga did such a nice job of microsurgery that I won't even end up with a scar as a souvenir." She gestured to her exposed abdomen, and Kirk saw the flesh-toned antiseptic patch on her. "He says I'll be fit for duty sometime tomorrow."

Kirk smiled and patted her shoulder. "How about the rest?" the captain asked, turning to McCoy.

"It was touch and go with several of them—those hand weapons leave nasty wounds—but we didn't lose one."

Kirk let out a long sigh of relief. "After the way I fouled up down there, that's at least one thing I don't have to feel guilty about."

"Do you know what your problem is?" McCoy said softly.

"Yes . . . I was too cocky," Kirk replied. "I took my men into a possible combat situation without adequately planning for contingencies. It's just a fluke that several of them weren't killed."

"Wrong answer," McCoy said. Kirk eyed him speculatively.

"Then what's the right one?"

"You're the best captain I've ever served under, except for one thing—you've somehow got yourself convinced that if the dice don't come out the way you want them to every time you roll them, you're to blame. No matter how carefully you plan, Jim, sometimes things just don't turn out the way they should. Unpredictables always creep in. And there isn't a general in history who hasn't lost a battle or two because of them. Mbenga and I were convinced we had the right formula for the paralysis drug, but evidently there are certain Vulcan physiological factors that we just didn't know about. There was no way you could know the drug would wear off in a few minutes. If it hadn't, we'd have had Spock up here now and be on our way at Warp Three."

"Maybe so," Kirk protested, "but—"

"But nothing," McCoy said impatiently. "A medical mistake was made. But Mbenga and I aren't sulking in our tents because of it." He gestured at the crowded sickbay. "We can't afford to; there's still too much work to be done. In the meantime, Spock is down there and we're up here, and it's up to you to do something about the situation, right?"

After a moment of silence, Kirk said tiredly, "You're right as usual, Bones. The first thing on the agenda is to try to find Spock's present location. The last thing I saw of him, he was disappearing down the street in that black wagon of his. I'm going to beam down and see what I can find out. How about a shot of something to clear my head and give me an energy boost? I'm so tired I can't think straight."

McCoy shook his head firmly. "The first item on your agenda is a decent night's sleep. You can hardly stand, and you've a long day ahead of you tomorrow. I'll send one of the survey party back down to check out the situation. My Rx for you is a double shot of brandy and bed." He grinned when Kirk started to protest. "You may be captain, Jim, but I'm the ship's surgeon. At times like this, you take orders from me. Bed! On the double!"

Kirk responded with a wan smile. "Aye, aye, sir," he said, "but I want to be awakened as soon as we get word of what's going on down there."

Minutes later he entered his cabin, stripped off his Kyrosian healer's robe, and threw it on the chair. Then, without even stopping to remove his boots, he tumbled into bed and fell into a deep, dreamless sleep.

He was wakened by a gentle shaking and the bracing smell of hot, black coffee. He opened his eyes blearily. Dr. McCoy was standing over him, holding out a large mug.

"Morning, Jim. Watch it, it's hot."

"What time is it?"

"07:00."

Kirk sat up so abruptly that he almost knocked the cup out of McCoy's hand.

"What happened? You were supposed to call me."

"There's bad news, but I figured you'd be better able to handle it after a good rest."

In a split second, Kirk was fully awake.

"What is it?"

"I sent Elkins down. He beamed back up shortly after midnight with word that there's hell to pay down there. Spock got back to his headquarters and sent out orders for all his people to assemble there. Those of his bodyguard who saw us flick out of sight were pretty shaken up. But he explained that as the work of demons from the stars who are trying to thwart his mission but were powerless against him." McCoy's tone grew grimmer.

"You know, Jim, using Kaseme's men seemed like a good idea at the time, but it's really backfired."

"How? Explain." Kirk demanded.

"Elkins heard everything. Spock's original plan was to enlist the city people and lead a combined crusade against the rest of Kyros. But after last night, his paranoid brain is convinced that all the Androsians have turned against him, so the city and its satellite villages are going to be the first targets. He's sent out orders for all the nearby clans to gather, and before too long they'll be riding out of the hills. Exosociology said they were never a threat to the city before because they were too busy fighting among themselves, but once Spock goes to work on them with that hypnotic voice of his, he's going to amass an army that'll top anything Mohammed ever commanded!"

"We'd better send another party down there right away!"

"And what do you propose to do with it once you get down?" McCoy said. "Our bird has flown the coop! The exiled clansmen rioted, on his orders, and in the process, burned down half that slum. While they were doing that, and keeping the soldiers and townspeople busy trying to control the burning, Spock and his bodyguards attacked the main gate. If that fancy cart of his hasn't broken a wheel, he's halfway to the hills by now."

"Damn it, Bones," Kirk exploded, "you should have wakened me! We might have thought of a way to stop him!"

"Impossible," McCoy said. "He was gone by the time Elkins heard about the breakout. What could you have done? Beam down and chase him on foot?"

Kirk didn't answer. Instead, he rose to his feet and punched the bridge call button on the communicator. "This is the captain . . . have all department heads report to the briefing room in forty-five minutes."

McCoy suddenly burst out laughing.

"What's so funny?" Kirk demanded.

McCoy pointed down. "Do you usually go to bed with your boots on? Rx this time is a cold shower and a clean uniform."

"Aye, aye, sir," Kirk said, as he lifted a foot and slowly inspected his Kyrosian half-boots. Then he sat and began to untie the complicated laces.

"Coffee, Captain?" a yeoman asked Kirk. He shook his head, and she passed down the briefing room table. Several officers selected cups. Kirk glanced at the chronometer on the wall: 10:45. They'd gotten a lot of work done in the last three hours. McCoy had been right; drugs were no substitute for sleep. Now he was able to view the previous day's events from a proper perspective. He glanced at a scribbled agenda on the table in front of him. He'd just checked off another item. Kirk looked at the small visual monitor on the table. It showed Ensign George propped up in a diagnostic bed; several sheets of paper lay about with hastily scrawled diagrams on them.

"Are you sure it will work?" Kirk asked.

The woman nodded confidently. "I know it will. Once it's switched on, it will jam the input stage of Spock's implant and cut his connection with Chag Gara. In theory, once that hill preacher's paranoia stops surging across, Spock will revert to his old self in no time at all. But I'm afraid he's going to be in for a few bad moments when he takes a Vulcan look at some of the things he's been doing the last few days."

"I don't like that 'in theory' part," McCoy muttered. "In theory, the telescan implant was supposed to have been thoroughly debugged, and look at the mess it got us into."

"Don't blame the implant, blame me," the girl said. "If I hadn't been so damn stupid . . ." Her voice trailed off.

"Ensign!" Kirk's voice was stern. "Self-recrimination is a luxury we can't afford at the moment. Is there any way to increase the range of that thing? The way it's presently designed, somebody's going to have to get close enough to Spock to almost touch him. And that raises certain practical difficulties."

Sara brought her attention back to the discussion.

"It's power supply has to be small enough so Mr. Spock can't detect it with that rigged tricorder. But that does give us an advantage; with subminiaturization, we'll be able to conceal it in a native bracelet where it'll be undetectable." She gestured at her healing stomach. "Tissue regeneration is almost complete, Dr. Mbenga told me, so I'll be out of here in a few hours and Lieutenant Uhura and I can get to work."

"Bones, will she be fit for duty soon?" Kirk asked.

"She'll be wobbly for a while, but otherwise she's as good as new."

"Good!" He glanced along the conference table. "Now, we need ideas on how to get close enough to Spock so that the nullifier can cut the link between him and that crazy preacher. Suggestions?"

"All I can think of are a lot of reasons why we can't," Uhura said.

"Scotty?"

"Naething in my department. If it was technology that was needed, my lads and I are sitting on top of the best the Federation has to offer. But we canna use it down there because of the divilish hob Spock has played with his tricorder."

"McCoy?"

"After yesterday's try, his followers aren't going to let anybody they don't like get within half a mile of him." He shook his head gloomily. "I don't know, Captain, I just don't know."

"Navigator?"

Chekov glanced at Kirk. "Mount a field phaser on a shuttlecraft and let me take it down," the young Russian said. "I'll find him and . . ."

"And have the tricorder self-destruct long before you got within firing range?"

"And what difference would that make?" Chekov demanded hotly. "We're going to have to abandon ship soon, the way it looks now. At least we can burn out that cancer before it can spread!"

"Mr. Chekov, you're here because it's part of your education as a Command staff officer," Kirk said. "If you ever hope to be a starship captain, you'll have to think of ways to preserve your ship and yourself. I suggest you start now."

Kirk glanced at the other officers and received only mute head shakes and shrugs to a second query for suggestions.

"I can sympathize with Chekov's feelings," he said, "but insane as he is, Spock knows that I know enough about history to realize that he is safe from direct attack. Killing him would make him a martyr; in a week there'd be stories that he rose from the dead and appeared among the faithful crying for vengeance. Stopping a living messiah is something we may yet do; a legend would unleash forces beyond anyone's control."

He paused and stared at the vacant chair where Spock customarily sat. "I don't think I've ever missed Spock—our old Spock—as much as I do right now. If he were sitting there, he'd wait until we all had our say and then cock a quizzical eyebrow and come out with a solution that would make us all feel like children, it would be so obvious and simple. But since we no longer have his Vulcan brain to rely on, we'll have to do the best we can with our human ones. We still have a little time left, and we have a device that will bring him back to normal if we can get close enough. So we'll try."

Kirk turned to the lieutenant commander in charge of exosociology. "Commander Dobshansky, are you familiar with the old tribal group on Earth—the Gypsies?"

The burly officer knit together gray brows and thought for a moment. "I remember something about them, sir. Why?"

"Because they were able to wander anywhere they wanted. No boundaries could stop them. A Frenchman in a small English village would have stuck out like a sore thumb, but Gypsies, being so widely scattered and relatively harmless, hardly excited comment. Are the Beshwa anything like that?"

"Beshwa? Let's see . . . Yes they are, come to think of it. They're sharp traders, good tinkers, fine musicians, and some have the reputation of being magical healers. They even travel around in caravans the way the Gypsies used to."

"I know," Kirk said. "McCoy and I saw one the other day in Andros. That's what gave me the idea. If we're going into the hills after Spock, we'll need a disguise that'll pass muster."

"You know, sir," Dobshansky said, "I think you've hit on something. This is the beginning of their trading season and a Beshwa cart wouldn't seem at all out of place in the hills. Shall I have the computer check the data banks to see what we've picked up on them so far?"

"By all means," Kirk said. "Bones, you said there were some Beshwa profiles among those that Sara took . . . How many?"

"Two," McCoy replied.

"Any reason two of us couldn't be hooked into the same dop?"

"None. All we need is access to language and behavioral patterns to be able to pass as the real thing."

"All right, then," Kirk said, "that gives us our identities. Transportation is next. Scotty, that should be your department. The Beshwa travel around in an odd-looking two-unit contraption, a sort of wagon in front with a high, closed van in the back—for sleeping, I suppose. They probably put trade goods in front. If we dig up some photographs, do you think you can build us one?"

The engineer frowned and shook his head. "I could gie you an exterior that might pass a hasty inspection, but not from too close. If I had blueprints . . . better yet, if an original could be beamed up, I'll have my lads make a duplicate that couldn't be told from the real thing."

"If we beamed up an original, we wouldn't need a duplicate," Kirk said dryly, "but I see your point. Mr. Chekov . . ."

The young Russian, who except for his one outburst, had been sitting quietly for most of the conference, looked up.

"Yes, sir?"

"More education. Trot down to Andros and pick us up a Beshwa wagon. There should be at least one loading for the summer trading."

With an effort, the navigator kept his face impassive.

"Yes, sir. Will there be anything else, sir?"

"You might pick up a liter of milk and a couple of dozen eggs on your way back." Kirk struggled to keep down his own smile.

"Yes, sir. Right away, sir." Chekov rose to his feet and marched stiffly to the door. When he reached it he paused, turned, and executed a flourishing salute.

" 'Theirs not to reason why,' " he declaimed dramatically.

" 'Theirs but to do and die.' " Grinning, Kirk completed the line.

"I thought our young friend only read Russian poetry," McCoy said.

"Well, it *is* a poem involving Russians," Kirk said, looking toward Chekov who stood at rigid attention. "His ancestors blew mine out of the saddle with their cannons during the Charge of the Light Brigade."

"What's a . . . light brigade?" Sulu asked bemusedly.

"Six hundred men on horses armed only with swords and pistols," Kirk explained. "Mr. Chekov seems to have stumbled on an old English poem called 'The Charge of the Light Brigade.' It's about an incident during the Crimean War between Russia and England when, through a typical piece of brass-hat idiocy, a British cavalry unit was charging into a valley lined with Russian guns. The point of the poem is that it's a glorious thing to get yourself killed because of a stupid order by a superior.

"All right, Ensign, I get the message. I suppose you'd like me to tell you how you're supposed to get hold of a Beshwa caravan?"

"No, sir," Chekov replied, still maintaining his rigid posture and a straight face. "A potential captain must be resourceful, sir. It is the milk and eggs that has me puzzled. My dop doesn't seem to have heard of either; there are no chickens or cows on Kyros."

There were several guffaws around the table, and Chekov relaxed.

"Then belay the groceries," Kirk said. "How do you propose to get the other item?"

"By buying it, sir," Chekov said smugly. "The Beshwa are traders, and a proper trader will sell his own mother if the price is right. I'll stop by Engineering and pick up a sack of Mr. Scott's counterfeit gold coins." Chekov began to leave.

"Wait," Kirk called. "Bones, what shape is Kaseme in?"

"Doped to the gills, Jim. He was given a shot before he recovered from his fainting spell last night, and he's been out ever since. Why?"

"He's got to be returned eventually. We'll let Mr. Chekov lug him down to the transporter." Kirk turned back to Chekov. "Tell Rogers to shift the co-ordinates, Ensign, and drop Kaseme in his own bedroom. If he remembers anything, he'll put it down to an alcoholic nightmare. Will you take care of that, Ensign?"

Chekov nodded and left.

"I've got a feeling that someplace along the line my navigator gave one of my legs a slight pull," Kirk said with a grin. " 'Their's not to reason why,' indeed. Well, let's get on to the next item on the agenda. Spock's location. Thanks to Lieutenant Uhura, we have a pretty good idea where he might be." Kirk turned to Uhura. "Lieutenant, if you please."

The black woman snapped an order to the computer, and on the briefing room's larger vision screen, a strange picture appeared. It was dark and punctuated by blobs and squiggles of light.

"The Captain and I were discussing Mr. Spock's whereabouts earlier, trying to figure a way to trace his movements. Once he got to the hills, there was no way of telling what direction he and his party might have taken. It occurred to me that our orbital scanners might have picked up some information."

She gestured to the large picture. "That is a nighttime infra-red scan of the Andros area," she explained.

"The white blotch at the bottom is Andros. Cities throw off a lot of heat, even at night. The wavy line along here is the coast; there's a marked temperature differential between land and sea."

She gave another order to the computer and a bright line crawled from Andros, moved halfway up the screen, and then arced left. "A time sequence of Spock and his riders," she said. "I thought a group that big, riding together, might generate enough heat to be picked up. I had no luck with the 1.3 and 2.2 micron windows, but hit paydirt on the 3.4. With a little computer enhancement, the slight trace I spotted was brought to what you see. Once the sun came up, the background thermal level rose to such a point that we lost him, but at least we know where he was at 06:00 this morning."

"Spock may have more brain power than any one of us," Kirk said as Uhura sat down. "But as a team we can't be beat."

He called an order to the computer, and the infra-red blow-up was replaced by a normal light photograph of the same area.

He stepped closer to the large screen. "If the clans respond to Spock's call for a holy war—and after his Afterbliss demonstration there's no doubt in my mind that they will—he's going to need a fairly large assembly ground. Just beyond where the infra-red track ends," Kirk pointed to the photo, "there's a large valley which opens onto the plains. That strikes me as a natural jump-off point for a strike on Andros. If Chekov gets us that Beshwa caravan, we'll beam down here—" he indicated a spot about thirty kilometers northeast of the city, "—and circle back through the hills so we can appear to have come in from the northeast."

"That's rough looking country," McCoy remarked. Kirk nodded.

The photo showed the sharp, jagged peaks of the mountain lairs of the hill clans; the lower foothills, slashed with gullies cut by the torrential spring rains, where they grazed their flocks from early summer through late fall; and finally the wide coastal plains that undulated down to the sea. The dominant feature of the aerial photo was a deep gorge that angled down from the northeast, cutting a twisting furrow through the foothills until it widened and discharged the river flowing on its bottom onto the plains. There the waters slowed, finally spreading out into a broad delta and joining the sea near Andros. The plain was criss-crossed with lines marking secondary roads connecting the agricultural villages, and broader ones showing main market roads leading to the city.

Kirk traced the road that went almost due north. When it reached the gorge, he paused.

"There's evidently a bridge across here, though the scale is too small to show it," he said. "You'll note that the road picks up on the other side. A few kilometers farther north is a mining settlement which is the source of most of Andros's iron. It is located by the mines, and up a ravine a few kilometers to the east, there's a crude smelter."

There was a groan from Scott. "I remember the place," he said sourly, "or rather my dop does. He spent a year of compulsory city service there when he was younger." Scott's personality seemed to disappear and be replaced by an even more crotchety, cynical one. "What a hole! No girls, one lousy wine shop that watered the juice so much it took four liters to get a buzz on, and typical army chow. Ugh!"

"Army?" Uhura said curiously.

"That's right, sweetie. It was a paramilitary operation, and still is. The clans always want to steal our spearstone, and every now and then they'll pull a sneak raid to grab off a few ingots. Nothing large scale," he added, "but enough of a nuisance so that only young men run the operation. What a pain! A week in the mines, a week at the smelter, a week on guard, and then you start the whole cycle over again. If I'd known, and had a choice, I would have picked the galleys!"

Scott stopped suddenly and looked sheepishly about.

"I mean my dop would. It's sair weird being able to tap into somebody else's memories at will. While you're doing it, you get to feeling you were there yourself."

"That's why the telescan implants seemed like such a great idea for survey use," McCoy said. "Though I myself felt from the start—"

"We're all aware of your feelings, Bones," Kirk said, "but the postmortem can wait. At the moment, we have only three days and a few odd hours left to save Kyros from a brutal, theocratic dictatorship ruled by a mad genius . . . and save our own necks and the *Enterprise* in the process." He turned back to the photograph displayed on the large vision screen and pointed again, continuing his briefing.

"Just north of the mining settlement is one of the main east-west migration trails of the hill people. We'll swing left there and approach from a less suspicious direction. Our best plan would be to join with one of the clans which is riding to join Spock, and journey along with them. A gathering that size would be a natural place for Beshwa to set up shop."

When the conference broke up a half hour later, the general structure of the plan to sever the link between Spock and Chag Gara had been worked out. Its keystone would be Ensign Sara George.

Well guarded as he was, Kirk realized, there was no way strangers could get close enough to Spock for the implant nullifier to be effective; but the gross sexuality he had inherited from his doppleganger, Chag Gara, might be his undoing. If . . .

There were too many *ifs* in the scheme, as Kirk was the first to point out. But the alternatives were unacceptable.

CHAPTER ELEVEN

It had been three hours since the meeting broke up. Captain Kirk was sprawled out on his bunk staring at the ceiling, his mind busily working on the details of the coming expedition, when the intraship communicator sounded. He rolled off the bunk.

"Kirk here."

"Sorry to bother, Jim," McCoy's voice said, "but we have a neelot problem. Can you come down to the cargo transporter?"

When he got to the transporter room, crewmen were wheeling a gaudily painted Beshwa wagon off the stage and over to one side. Chekov, a miserable expression on his face, was braced against the control console, his Kyrosian shorts down around his ankles. McCoy finished applying an antiseptic spray to one bare buttock, then sprayed a layer of flesh-colored foam that hardened into a thin, flexible sheet.

"There," he said. "In a couple of days the dermolastic will dry up and fall off, leaving a nice, pink gluteus."

"What happened to you?" Kirk demanded with a grin.

Chekov pulled up his shorts and turned so that Kirk could see a jagged tear in their seat.

"Damn neelot bit me, sir."

"His not to reason why," McCoy put in softly.

"So where is it . . . them?" the captain asked.

"Still down there, sir. While I was trying to hitch one of them to the wagon, he let loose with a kick that could have taken off my head if I hadn't jumped back out of range. When I did, another one just reached around and took a sample. Is it true that once they've tasted blood—"

"I'll see that you're mentioned in the log . . . sometime," Kirk interrupted. "However, we've now got a Beshwa caravan and nothing to pull it with."

"That's what happens when you send a boy to do a man's job," McCoy drawled. "Especially a city boy."

"I can't help it if my dop isn't a neelot tamer," Chekov said defensively. "I'd like to see what you would have done if you were in my shoes . . . sir."

McCoy made a modest gesture. "Once I'd shown them who was boss," he said, "they'd be eating out of my hand. As an old Georgia farm boy raised around Missouri mules, I've yet to see a meaner, more ornery critter than a terrestrial jackass, in spite of all the planets I've been to."

"Well," said Kirk, folding his arms across his chest, "it looks like we have a volunteer, doesn't it, Ensign?"

"Yes, sir!" came Chekov's enthusiastic reply.

"Now, wait just one little old second, Jim," McCoy protested.

Kirk looped his arm through one of McCoy's and escorted him to the transporter stage. "Shouldn't be any trouble at all for an 'old Georgia farm boy.'" He turned to the officer behind the control console. "Lieutenant, energize, if you please."

With a huge grin on her face, the woman officer did so.

"Yours not to reason why," Kirk called gaily as McCoy faded from sight in the glitter of the carrier wave.

Ten minutes later, the chief medical officer reappeared with six docile neelots in tow. "I was waiting a full five minutes," he said, as he led the animals to the wagon and rapidly hitched them up. Kirk noticed that his right knuckles were bruised and bleeding.

"Was that . . . eating *out of* your hand, or eating *of* it?" he asked.

"Couldn't find an ax handle, so I had to use my fist," McCoy explained. "They may have heads that look like alligators, but they're soft. A proper Missouri mule would have reared back and hee-hawed." Crooking his finger, and with a mock evil grin he said to Chekov, "Come along, Ensign. I wouldn't want you to get hoof and mouth disease at a time like this. I have an old-fashioned needle . . ."

Sometime later, Kirk, programmed with a Beshwa dop, lay on his bunk again and began to sample the store of knowledge of his new identity. He had become accustomed to the Androsian mind he was previously linked to, but the Beshwa were products of a different culture. As he gingerly began to probe the memories and attitudes of his dop, the communicator sounded.

This time it was his chief engineer.

"What's the problem, Scotty?"

"It's this Beshwa caravan," Scott explained. "I just canna make sense of some of its parts . . ."

Kirk grinned and realized he could get one up on his engineer because of his Beshwa dop.

"Hang on, Scotty, I'll be right down."

When he arrived in the cargo transporter room, which he had left only an hour before, he found his engineer standing by the odd-looking wagon, fists on hips, muttering softly.

"Can I be of any help?" Kirk asked innocently.

"Well, sir," Scott said, "if you can tell me why the wagon tongue is hinged so it can stick straight up in the air, and why the van can be disconnected from the wagon in front and, aboove all, why the blazes there's a telescoping boom twenty meters long and connecting the twa parts . . . I'll . . . I'll nae take a drink for a month!"

"You don't mean that?" Kirk asked in mock surprise. Scott nodded.

"Well," Kirk began, "even though I'm not an engineer, of course, it seems simple to me. I imagine the reason the two parts can be disconnected is so the Beshwa, if they have several short trading visits to make in one day, can unhook the van and park it somewhere convenient. As for the rest . . ."

Scott's jaw dropped farther and farther as Kirk went into a detailed explanation of the use of the various special features.

When he finished, he added modestly, "I may be way off base, though, Mr. Scott."

Scott turned wide eyes on his captain. "But you're right, Captain. That's the way it has to be. Now, why couldn't I have seen that?"

"Because I have a Beshwa dop and you don't, Scotty. Now, get down to sickbay and have Dr. McCoy link you into yours, and then you can check this caravan over thoroughly. We're beaming down before dawn tomorrow, and I don't want a wheel coming off the first hour on the road."

Scott turned to go, then swung back. "Captain, aboot that pledge . . ."

"Scotty," Kirk said, "do you really think I would make you go on the wagon?" Kirk grinned. Relieved, Scott went to sickbay.

Early the following morning, the landing party lined up before the Beshwa caravan for a quick inspection. The experiment of hooking two men into one dop had worked out well; the only thing that betrayed the overlapping was when the officers went into character. In spite of their physical differences, in intonations and mannerisms Kirk and Chekov were almost like identical twins. The same was true for Scott and McCoy, who had been double linked to the other Beshwa profile in the medical department files. Only Sara, still a little pale from her ordeal but otherwise in good shape, remained linked to her original doppleganger, the amorous little Androsian belly dancer; but since Beshwa women were retiring sorts who took no part in the trading, it was hoped she would be able to pass virtually unnoticed. In her case, her nonverbal abilities were considered more important than her verbal, though she had been given a quick hypno-briefing on Beshwa patois the night before, and her dop, for business reasons, already had a fair command of the hill tongue.

The caravan had contained enough clothing to outfit them all—Chekov's purse had been large enough to buy the vehicle just as it stood, complete with dirty crockery from the morning meal of the former owners.

The men wore gaudily decorated leather tunics that stretched to their knees. Over them they wore sleeveless leather jackets with V-shaped openings that plunged from neck to waist, and woven trousers. Their hair, now dyed a purplish black, had been shaved on each side so that only a five-centimeter-wide strip remained. They were unarmed, in accordance with Beshwa tradition. Their skins had been darkened to a deep mahogany color, and their contact lenses were slightly more pinkish than the Kyrosian norm.

Sara's dress was similar to the men's, except that instead of hanging loosely, her tunic fit her voluptuously curved body like a second skin; and her hair, also dyed, had been trimmed to a pert page-boy bob.

Kirk surveyed the small party closely, then nodded his head in approval. "All aboard," he called. He and Chekov climbed into the driver's seat on the wagon, as the others scrambled up to perch on the trade goods on the wagon's bed. They seated themselves comfortably on the thick fur covering.

"Energize," Kirk ordered.

The neelots hissed and reared nervously, as they suddenly felt earth under their hooves instead of the ridged plate of the cargo transporter. Kirk's newly acquired driver's skill was put to a severe test as he tried to keep them from bolting. After he had them quieted down, he looked around, attempting to determine their location.

Dim shapes that seemed like bushes humped around them, but all the moons had set, and starshine didn't provide enough light for traveling safely. A half hour passed before a faint grayness began to appear on the eastern horizon. When at last it was light enough, Kirk jumped down from the wagon and pushed through tangled vegetation, Sara at his heels, until he came to an outcropping of rock which jutted ten meters into the air. When he reached the rock, he clambered up it, and slowly surveyed the surrounding countryside.

"We seem to be right on target," he said as he reached down to help Sara climb up beside him.

To the north he could make out an escarpment slashing across the middle distance. It rose to the far left rather abruptly and cut east, separating the foothills from the plains. Along its base ran a gorge, deeply cut into living rock by millennia of rushing waters. Directly ahead, a roaring sounded in the distance, and the first rays of Kyr gave rainbow tints to a cloud of dancing mist that rose above the canyon's edge to signal a waterfall below.

He swung one hundred and eighty degrees and faced due south, studying the wind-scoured plains which sloped gently down toward Andros and the sea. There was no sign of life. He looked back in the direction they were to travel.

"Can you make out the bridge, Captain?" Sara asked.

He shook his head and glanced back in the direction of Andros.

The rolling country dotted with brush, barren as it was, seemed almost benign compared to the rugged foothills and the roaring chasm ahead.

He was about to climb down from his vantage point when a light morning wind shifted and the mist was rolled back.

"There it is," he exclaimed. "I can just make out the top ends of the support poles. It's not far off."

"Why couldn't we have beamed down farther back?" Sara asked, as they headed back to the Beshwa caravan.

"The migration path we'll be taking to cut in behind Spock's gathering is fairly heavily traveled. It might have looked a little odd if a Beshwa caravan suddenly appeared in the middle of a clan heading for their summer grazing grounds. This way, if we run into any hillmen when we reach the trail, we can simply say that we turned down to the mining settlement for some trading."

When they arrived at their strange, many-wheeled vehicle, McCoy poked his head out of the back door of the van, where he and the rest had taken refuge from the morning chill.

"Do you have us located?" the doctor asked.

Kirk nodded. "The road from Andros is just to the left, and the bridge is almost straight ahead."

They cut through the brush and then down a hill until they reached the dirt road. It was rutted from heavy traffic, though there was no one on it at the moment. As they traveled along, slightly below the level of the rolling country they had just left, the bridge's support poles began to rise from behind a low hill. When they topped it, Kirk pulled the neelots to a halt and stared down in dismay.

The heavy *jakim* cables which should have arced between the uprights to support the suspension bridge, dangled loosely into the ravine between.

Kirk whipped the neelots forward, and the wagon lumbered quickly to the edge of the gorge. Halting it, Kirk leaped down.

The bridge was gone; the only link between the hills and the lowlands for forty kilometers in either direction lay in tangled ruins at the bottom of the canyon.

Kirk raised his eyes and peered to the opposite side. The cables had been cut from the far side and, like a taut ribbon cut at one end, the bridge had gone curling into the depths below. The party stood looking for a moment at the now inaccessible road on the other side that wound back into the hills; and then they turned and went back to the vehicle.

"Why?" Sara murmured.

Kirk dug into the memory of his dop.

"Spearstone, It looks like the clans are already on the move." He pointed toward the sharply rising hills on the other side of the ruined bridge. "Back that way about six kilometers is the source of most of Andros's iron. There are some rich veins there. Spock's working fast. The first step in a major offensive is to cut off the raw materials your enemy needs for instruments of war." Kirk turned around and faced Chekov.

"Get me the map, Ensign. There must have been a way to get across before the bridge was built."

The Russian went into the caravan and emerged a moment later with a roll of parchment-like material.

Kirk unrolled it and spread it out on a flat rock. He
studied it for a long moment, his face clouded in con-
centration. Finally, he put a finger on the map.

"Look," he said, his finger tracing a path. "A few
kilometers downstream, the gorge river empties into a
small lake. I'll bet in the old days the iron was ferried
across. I don't know how they'd get it out otherwise.
The terrain on the far end of the lake looks even more
rugged than it is along here. If my hunch is right, there
should be an old road branching off not too far back
which we can take down to the lake."

"What do we do when we get there?" Sara asked.
"Swim to the other side? Somehow I doubt that the
ferry is still running."

Kirk grinned at the officer. "We're Beshwa, remember? We go where we want, even when there aren't any
convenient bridges around." He stood up, rolling the
map. "You'll see," he added cryptically.

There was a road. But it was so overgrown with
vegetation that they almost missed it. As they jolted
down the old trail, they had to stop at intervals and
hack a path wide enough for the caravan to pass
through the thickets which had grown up since the
road was last used. Nearly an hour later, the Beshwa
vehicle emerged from a narrow ravine onto a bank that
sloped gently down to the edge of a placid lake. Sara
ran to the shore, knelt, cupped her hands, and splashed
cold, clear water on her sweaty, dust-grimed face.
"Umm," she called, "that's lovely. Is there time for a
quick swim, Captain?"

"Go ahead," Kirk said. "Since you don't have a
Beshwa dop, you won't be much help rigging the caravan."

Sara stripped off her clothes without a hint of self-
consciousness, ran out onto a long flat rock which jutted over the lake's edge, and then, like a golden naiad,
arced into the cool water.

"You know, Jim," McCoy chuckled and said, "no
matter how this crazy expedition ends up, I don't think
Sara will ever go back to being her old, prim self."

"If this expedition is ever going to go anyplace,"

Kirk said, "we'd better get to work. Scotty, you and Chekov unhitch the neelots. Bones and I will disconnect the van and wagon."

Not long after, the job was done. The long wagon tongue, hinged where it was connected to the front of the wagon, now stood erect, a sturdy mast. A timber had been attached about a third of the way up tho tongue to serve as a boom, and the canvas-like covering that protected the trade goods in the wagon was ready to be rigged as a sail.

"Sara," Kirk called to the woman, who was happily cavorting in the water a hundred meters out, "we're ready to launch. Come in and keep an eye on the neelots, while we take the van and the cargo across."

As she came flashing toward them, like a graceful mermaid, the four men put their shoulders to the back of the van and rolled it down the slope into the water. Then, as it bobbed gently like a great floating box, they went back and rolled down the wagon.

"Can I help?" called Sara, as she pulled herself onto a sun-warmed rock, as unconcerned about her nudity as a child.

"Now you can," Kirk replied. He removed his neelot-hide boots and waded out to where the van and the wagon floated a few meters apart. "You can give me a hand getting these two hooked together." She dove back into the water and surfaced at his side. He reached under the front of the van and took hold of the protruding end of the telescoping pole. He pulled it out a few meters and then slid the tip into a socket at the rear of the floating wagon, locking it into place with a metal pin.

"Push the wagon on out until this thing's fully extended," he said. "I'll set the locking pins at each of the joints."

Sara dug her feet into the sand of the gently shelving bottom, and pushed the van out into the lake until the rod was fully extended.

"That's it," Kirk said as he moved toward her, reaching under water at each junction of the sections to lock it in place. "We're ready to go."

"I guess it's a boat now," Sara said. "But why break it into two parts?"

"The van's so high," Kirk answered, "it would cut off most of the wind. It's a stubby mast. Why don't you untether the neelots and water them? They're probably as thirsty as we."

The girl nodded, swam back to the rock, and slipped into her clothes. McCoy and the rest waded out and climbed up on the wagon. Scott broke into an off-key rendition of "Anchors Aweigh," as Kirk hoisted the sail and let the boom swing out until it was almost at right angles to the wagon. Slowly, as the wind bellied out the one-piece canvas-like covering, the strange craft began to gather momentum. The van rode decorously behind, kept in position by the long, flexible connecting pole.

"Ready on the brake, Bones," Kirk said as the front wheels made contact with the shelving bottom of the opposite shore, and the wagon began to roll up out of the water. When it was far enough inland so the van also was beached, McCoy brought the vehicle to a halt.

Chekov jumped down and released the connecting rod from its socket, telescoping each section until all of it had slid back into its protective tunnel under the van. In the meantime, Kirk and the other two dropped the tailgate of the wagon and were busily unloading bundles of trade goods.

When the wagon was finally empty, McCoy released the brake and it went sailing down the beach, entering the water at an angle as Kirk tacked into the northerly wind. Once across the small lake, they loaded the neelots into the now empty wagon and again set sail for the opposite shore.

It took an hour of arduous brush-hacking before they finally got back onto the main road. Before it had seemed like only a rutted cart trail, but compared to what they had been over on their detour, it was more like a broad highway.

When they were almost at the top of a long slope, Kirk turned the reins over to McCoy and unrolled the map.

"We should reach the Androsian mining settlement in a couple of hours," he said. "Once over the crest, the road doglegs into a narrow canyon. The mines and the workers' huts are located where it widens out. The smelter is up a side canyon near a stream that supplies water for its operation." He raised his eyes from the map and rolled it closed. "Beshwa have been here before, so this will be the first test of how well we'll be able to pass."

"That will be no problem, Captain," said a confident voice from the rear. Kirk turned. Chekov had made a comfortable nest with carefully arranged bundles and a soft fur blanket. He sprawled indolently. "As long as we have our dops to cue us, nobody will be able to tell us from the real thing."

"Except for Sara," Scott said. "She isnae linked to a Beshwa."

Chekov chortled. "Sara doesn't need a Beshwa dop. As long as there are males around, our little belly dancer will be able to handle the situation. Right, little *vabushka?*" he said, reaching over as if to pat her firmly rounded rump.

"Ensign George to you, if you please," she said. "And keep your hands to yourself. My dop doesn't engage in erotic play with children."

Chekov's retort was cut off by a sudden roll of thunder. Dark storm clouds were piling up over the mountains to the west and rapidly moving toward them.

"Looks like another soaker coming up," Kirk said. "That radiation front is really screwing up Kyros's weather. Better get in the van; no point in all of us getting wet."

For the next hour the caravan crawled through the beating rain, climbing steadily up the road that snaked along the bottom of the winding canyon that led through the hills to the mining settlement. Finally the rain tapered off; and when Kirk stopped to rest the neelots, the others came out of the van and climbed back into the wagon.

"Dismal territory," Kirk remarked.

The surrounding foothills were even more tumbled,

rough, and rock-and-bush-strewn than they had appeared in the photos taken by the automatic survey cameras aboard the *Enterprise*. The sky was sullen gray, pregnant with dark, swollen thunderheads. Shivering, Kirk slapped the reins and urged the neelots into motion.

When another hour had passed, they seemed to have almost reached the crest of the range of hills. The cloud cover had lightened considerably, parting occasionally to let a watery sun appear.

Suddenly McCoy gripped Kirk's arm.

"Look, Jim," he said, pointing. "Over there, a little to the left. Isn't that smoke?"

"It's probably just mist."

McCoy sniffed the air. "Mist never smelled like that," he said. "There's something burning ahead."

Kirk took a whip from its socket beside the seat and cracked it over the neelots' heads. They broke into a loose-jointed canter. When the caravan finally topped the crest of the hill and Kirk saw what lay ahead, he jerked back sharply on the reins, bringing the caravan to a sudden halt.

"What's going on?" Sara's voice called from the rear.

"Stand up and see," Kirk replied grimly. "Spock must be already on the march."

A gusting wind, moaning dirge-like from the mountains, carried smoke and the smell of slaughter to the stunned travelers. Kirk sat, staring down at the scene of carnage. McCoy rose partway from his seat, his mouth open, and Chekov stared, shock scrawled across his boyish face. Only Scott spoke.

"Great Lord of Space . . ."

CHAPTER TWELVE

From the point where the caravan stood, the road ran in switchbacks down a steep hill. At the bottom stretched the smoking ruins of a small village. Kirk sat unmoving for a long minute. Nothing stirred below. Finally, he released the brake and guided the caravan down the twisting road, stopping at last at a half-open gate in the stockade that surrounded the village.

It creaked slightly on its hinges, swinging slowly forward and then back as it was caught by gusts of wind. Hanging from it, pinioned grotesquely, was the spear-skewered body of a young Androsian in military dress. Several more bodies stood in military array against the palisade walls on each side of the gate, held erect by swords, their own swords, which had been pounded through their chests into the wood behind like giant nails.

Kirk tapped the reins and the caravan moved slowly through the gate. As the wind blew it almost shut again, the blank eyes of the dead man pinned to the portal seemed to follow them accusingly.

They moved along a deserted street into a small central square. Around it were smoldering ruins that once had been barracks and store houses. Hacked bodies lay where they had fallen, already enveloped by buzzing clouds of flies.

Kirk halted by a central well which was ringed by a meter-high parapet. Propped against it, hands and feet bound behind them, were a dozen headless bodies. Chekov climbed down and peered over the edge at the blood-tinged water only a meter below.

"Their eyes are open," he said, "and they all seem to be looking up. I thought when you died your eyes closed like when you are going to sleep."

"Not when you die that way," McCoy said. He had to help Chekov back into the wagon.

"I think I'm going to be sick," Sara murmured.

Kirk knew what she was thinking. One impulsive act—and this!

"Let's get out of here," he said harshly. "There's nothing we can do about what happened here. But maybe we can stop any more of it from happening." He pulled the neelots to one side to swerve around a corpse sprawled in the middle of the street, gashed throat gaping at the sky like a horrible second mouth.

"Jim," McCoy said suddenly, "do you notice anything odd about all of this?"

The other shook his head. "There was no quarter given, and they cut the throats of all the wounded. But taking prisoners isn't the hill way."

"Tap deeper into your Beshwa memories, Jim. During all the years your dop traded among the clans, did he ever encounter anything like a funeral service?"

Kirk frowned, searched back through alien memories, and then shook his head. "No, come to think of it. I wonder why?"

"My dop," McCoy said, "was with a group of hillmen once when an old chief dropped dead—coronary, I imagine. They just walked away and left him crumpled on the ground. When my dop asked why, they said that what the spirit left behind was just dead meat which had no connection with the person that had been. That's what's odd about this. Hillmen have always left their dead where they fell, but this time they took their dead with them. And there must have been a number of them. The lads here didn't just stand like sheep and let themselves be slaughtered."

"It must be Spock's doing," Kirk replied. "The cultural changes are already beginning."

The gate at the north side of the village was also open, and they went through it and shortly reached a fork. The good road veered west into a canyon. The one that continued on north was little better than a cart track.

"Which way?" McCoy asked.

"Straight ahead," Kirk said. "The one to the left goes up a canyon to the smelter. No point in checking up there. There'd be more of the same. About a kilometer ahead we should hit the east-west migration trail. We swing left there." He turned in his seat. "You, back there. If we run into any hillmen, we know nothing about what happened back there. Say that we came from the northeast." Scott and the rest nodded. After what they had just seen, nobody felt in a conversational mood, especially Ensign George.

The migration trail wasn't an actual road but rather a wide track that ran along the bottom of a shallow valley; occasional rings of blackened stone marked places where hill clans and their herds had camped for the night during their annual migrations. Kirk breathed a sigh of relief as they moved westward, making good time over the relatively smooth ground. With luck, he thought, they would reach the Messiah's encampment sometime the next day.

They had only proceeded for a short distance when a warning cry came from Scott, who had jumped out of the wagon a few minutes before and was jogging alongside to exercise his cramped legs.

"Clansmen behind us! They're turning in from the road that leads back to the village."

Kirk swung the caravan half around and looked back along the trail. A party of riders, spear points glittering in the sun, was coming out of the canyon mouth that opened onto the trail a kilometer or so back. Behind them came a long line of heavily laden carts and several more riders, leading neelots bearing some kind of a burden.

"A raiding party," Kirk said. "They must have hit the smelter while the main group took the village and destroyed the bridge."

Suddenly, the riders in front broke into a gallop, leaving the main column behind as they came riding up the trail toward the caravan.

"It looks like we're about to have company," Kirk said quietly. "Everybody stay in character. Think Beshwa, act Beshwa, be Beshwa. Your dops will let you know how to behave. Sara, duck around the far side and get into the wagon. Stay there until I tell you to come out."

As the hillmen came galloping up, Kirk and the rest got down and stood in a line alongside the wagon, palms outstretched in greeting and bowing from the waist.

This greeting wasn't returned. Instead, as the masked neelot riders pulled to a halt, spears were lowered until their barbed points were only centimeters from the chests of Kirk and the rest.

"Beshwa greetings, honorable warriors," Kirk said with a welcoming smile. "Once again we move among your hills in search of trade, unmasked men with open hearts who bear no arms. If you return to your tents, may we join you? It will be good to camp again with old friends from the hills. We have new songs, new tales, and new wares. The first two are free, and the last is brought more for friendship than for profit."

There was no softening of the red eyes that glared down through mask eye slits. One of them turned to a rider who sat to one side, a black banner with a white circle flapping from his lance.

"Are these to be killed?"

The clansman addressed said, "Tram Bir ordered that all who were not of the folk were to be slain. Behead them."

Kirk stepped forward. "An act worthy of warriors," he said scornfully. "We bear no arms. When you ride home with our heads, will you boast of the fierce battle you had taking them?"

"All strangers are to die. It has been ordered," replied the first clansman.

"But we aren't strangers. Every summer since the time before there was time, we have come trading in these hills. Did your chief list the Beshwa among those who were to taste your steel?"

"No," said the rider slowly, "but—"

"Then take us to him," Kirk interrupted. "If we are to die, we are to die; but let it be at his words, once he sees who we are."

There was a silence that seemed to last an eternity. Finally, the rider shrugged. "I will ask his son. I would not have the blood of Beshwa or women on my hands, unless it was so ordered."

The rider turned his neelot and galloped back along the trail to the main column, which was now only a few hundred meters away. Its leader was slumped forward in his saddle. A rough bandage was wrapped around his hooded head and the right side of his battle cloak was blood-soaked. Behind him stretched a long procession of wagons, piled high with rough-cast iron ingots. On each side rode warriors, some also bandaged, some of them leading neelots with dead warriors trussed to them.

There was a momentary conversation, and then the rider trotted back.

"Alt says to take you to Tram Bir." He beckoned to two of the mounted tribesmen. They dismounted from their neelots and came over. "Bind them and put them in their wheeled house."

Chekov was first. He started to struggle as his arms were trussed behind his back, but he subsided when Kirk gave him a warning hiss. Then his feet were tied and he was dragged to the back of the van. One of the clansmen pulled open the rear door and peered inside.

"Hey, Chief," he yelled. "Come look what I found. There's a woman in here." He jumped inside the van and dragged Sara out into the light. "A pretty one, too," he said, running his eyes over her curves. "How about putting the others up front in the wagon and letting me ride back here?"

The leader shook his head. "Alt's orders were to take them to his father unharmed. Tie the girl and put her back with the rest." Grumbling, the hillman complied.

Kirk was the last to be dumped through the door. It was then slammed shut.

McCoy let out his breath in a long *whew*. "That was a close one," he said. "But at least Chekov kept his mouth shut for a change."

"Where do we go from here?" Sara asked.

"Wherever they want to take us," Kirk replied. "I

don't think we have much choice in the matter." The caravan lurched and began to roll forward on the trail.

"At least we're going in style," McCoy added. "We seem to have acquired a chauffeur."

They jolted along for half an hour, and then the caravan came to a stop. Somebody barked a command from the outside, and the rear door was pulled open. Hillmen reached in, dragged them out, and tossed them roughly on the ground. Kirk struggled to a sitting position, blinking as his eyes accustomed themselves to the outside brightness, and looked around.

Off to one side, at least a hundred neelots were staked out, several with dead bodies tied to their backs. Groups of hillmen were squatting around small fires, roasting chunks of dried meat on green sticks. A short distance from the caravan, Kirk saw a squat, bandy-legged figure whose hood and battle cloak bore the distinctive markings of a clan chief. He stood with his hands behind his back, staring off into the distance, seemingly oblivious to the bustle around him. The leader of the party that brought the Beshwa caravan in went over to him, saluted, and said something. The chief glanced at the bound captives and then back along the trail at the approaching carts and their escorts.

"Good," he grunted. "They bring more spearstone than I expected. The Messiah will be pleased. How many dead?"

"Six. Those plains sheep have sharp teeth."

"My son, did he fight well?"

"Like a man of twice his years. He killed four before a spear thrust brought him down. We wanted to bring him back in a cart, but he insisted on riding with the rest."

"And these?" The chief gestured toward Kirk and the rest.

"Beshwa. We found them on the trail."

"I know they're Beshwa, idiot. Why were they brought here?"

"Alt ordered it. He said that perhaps the Messiah's

order didn't apply to them. Beshwa have always been allowed to move freely through the hills."

"What has been, is past," the chief said harshly. "They are not of our blood. Kill them."

"The woman, too?"

Tram Bir nodded. As he turned to go, a stocky warrior beside him who wore the markings of a sub-chief held out a restraining hand and whispered something. The chief shrugged.

"Bring that one here," he ordered, pointing at Sara. Two hillmen jerked her to her feet and dragged her forward. Tram Bir eyed her critically. "She has a pretty face, Greth, but there doesn't seem to be much meat on her bones."

The sub-chief gave a coarse laugh. "We'll see," he said, and drew a razor-edged dagger from a sheath.

Kirk fought to keep control, frantically searching the memory of his Beshwa dop for some scrap of information about clan ways that could be used to stay the hillman's blade. Suddenly, he thought he had something. Superstition might work where argument wouldn't.

"Azrath!" he boomed in as deep a voice as he could manage, lifting his face to the sky. "Azrath, hear! They would harm your handmaiden!"

"What is this nonsense?" Tram Bir demanded in an irritated voice.

"She has been consecrated to Azrath. The power she draws from him will shield us all from harm. Why do you think the Beshwa bear no arms? Why do robber clans let the Beshwa pass in peace?" Kirk fixed his eyes directly on Tram Bir's. "If you touch our sister, Azrath's wrath will follow you and your children and your children's children. Your seed will be cursed until the end of time."

"That might have been true once," Tram Bir said coldly. "But we no longer fear foreign gods. We are the chosen of the Messiah."

"And your sister is to be chosen by the son of the chief—if he likes what he sees," Greth added in a mocking voice. He lowered his knife into the vee neck of Sara's short leather tunic, edge out, and slashed down suddenly. She struggled futilely against the hard grip of grinning guards on each side, as the chief's son pulled her slit garment open and exposed her shapely body to his father's eyes.

"See," he said, "there's lots of meat on those bones."

"Not enough for my taste," Tram Bir said, "but you can take her back with you if you want to. Just see that you dispose of her before we leave for the gathering in the morning. As for those—" he gestured toward the male captives—"cut their throats."

CHAPTER THIRTEEN

Clansmen pounced on and rolled the defenseless captives onto their backs. Knives lifted and were about to slash down, when there was a sudden shout.

"Chief, look! Your son Alt!"

A neelot was coming toward the group, a boyish figure slumped in the saddle, head hanging and eyes closed. The side of his mount glistened red where blood had run down it. The rider came to a stop a few meters from the chief and tried to straighten up.

"Father and chieftain, your orders have been carried out," the boy said in an almost inaudible, faltering voice. "I tried to do you honor in the fight and . . . and . . ." His voice died away and he started to fall sideways. Hands caught him and lowered him gently to the ground. His father knelt beside him and opened the boy's battle cloak. Extending from his side was a short length of broken spear shaft. The chief reached out his hand as if to grasp it, and then drew back.

"Hestor," he said, looking up. "Can this be removed?"

A stooped man with an elder's markings on his clan hood knelt beside Tram Bir. He took hold of the spear shaft and tugged at the splintered stub. The boy bit his lips and unsuccessfully tried to stifle a scream. Then he coughed and a bloody froth appeared.

"It's barbed," said the older man, rising to his feet. "It cannot be removed. It would be useless to let the boy suffer any longer."

For a moment, the chief gazed silently at his dying son. Then he reached down and drew a short, wide-bladed dagger from a sheath marked with ceremonial designs. He touched the tip of the blade to the boy's

125

throat and said in a low voice, "I offer my son to the Messiah. He dies a warrior's death. At the appointed time, may he be lifted to Afterbliss with the rest."

There was a hushed silence as he lifted the blade, and then a voice said quietly, "Our lives for his, Tram Bir. I can save your son."

The chief turned his head toward the prisoners. "The spear is barbed," he said harshly.

"Be that as it may," McCoy said, "I can heal him. But it must be done quickly. He bleeds inside. Soon it will be too late."

Tram Bir shook his head and turned back to his son.

"Beshwa have strange powers," said the elder who had examined the boy's wound. "Long ago they healed me of a fever when all else had failed."

Tram Bir considered the advice silently for a moment. At last, slowly replacing the ceremonial dagger in its sheath, he rose to his feet.

"If it is as you say, old friend, they shall earn my gratitude. If it isn't, they shall die . . . but not swiftly. Unbind them."

Moments later, the now unconscious boy was lifted into the van and laid on one of the built-in bunks. Sara, holding her slit tunic together with one hand, climbed in, followed by McCoy.

"You two wait out here," Kirk said to Chekov and Scott. He stepped up into the van and shut the door.

"All right, Bones," he said, "how are you going to get out of this?"

McCoy seemed strangely unperturbed. "We're still alive, aren't we, Jim? Since your Azrath didn't bail us out, somebody had to."

"For how long?"

"Just watch. If you thought for one moment that I, a Starfleet surgeon, was going to land on a planet two thousand years behind the Federation in medical technology and rely only on their herbs and potions, you are out of your star-picking mind."

Leaving Kirk standing with his mouth open, McCoy went to the front of the van and, bending down, opened a small, concealed panel. Reaching in a hand, he drew out a standard-issue Starfleet medikit.

"Did you think I was going to operate with a dirk and no antiseptics, Jim?" he asked blandly.

Before Kirk could answer, there was an imperious knocking at the van door. "Open up," called Tram Bir from outside, "I wish to be with my son."

"Sorry, honored chief," Kirk replied through the door, "but our spells won't work if you are present. We'll call you when we're through."

Tram Bir growled and went away.

McCoy gave the unconscious boy a shot of anesthetic and then straightened. "That should keep him under until I get the job done," he said. "I'm going to need your help in a minute, Jim, but first I've got to take a crash course in Kyrosian anatomy."

He switched on a medical tricorder and began to scan the boy's body.

"Heartbeats fluttering," he muttered, "—he has two, both tri-chambered—liver function normal, gastro-intestinal OK, lung—only one of those but as big as the two we have—severe trauma. Massive laceration of muscles and blood vessels, of course, but actually it looks worse than it is. This will take some time, though."

Then, moving the instrument to the boy's head, he continued, "Minor head wound, mild concussion." Glancing up at Kirk, he said, "Jim, get that hood off and staunch the blood while I work on this." He gestured at the broken spear shaft.

"Hold it," Kirk said. "If we're going to make this look really impressive, we ought to have atmosphere." He went to a chest and took out two native instruments, an oddly shaped horn that looked like a flat-iron with a hose attached to one end and a lute-like instrument with strings going in all directions. He went to the door, opened it a crack, and passed the instruments out to Scott and Chekov.

"Give us some music to make magic by," he muttered. "I don't care if it comes out sour, but I want it loud." As he shut the door and locked it, there was a brief moment of cacophony as the two officers struggled to agree on pitch, tune, and tempo; and then, somewhat off-key, the morbid strains of the "Saint James Infirmary Blues" resounded through the hills for the first time in the history of Kyros.

"Isn't that a violation of General Order One?" McCoy asked sourly, wincing at the raucous intermingling of toots and tweedles.

Kirk grinned. "Who's going to report us?"

"Well, if you can stand that racket, I guess I can. Let's get started. Get that hood off and clean up the head wound."

"Aye, sir," Kirk said. He untied the thongs holding the boy's headgear on and tried to pull it off. He couldn't. McCoy, seeing the trouble Kirk was having, handed him a scalpel.

"Cut it off," he said. Kirk carefully slit the hood from chin to forehead and then, bit by bit, peeled it back on both sides until it was free. Sara handed him a moistened sterilized pad from the medikit. He pressed it gently to the wound and began mopping away the congealed blood.

McCoy's fingers probed lightly around the broken spear shaft that protruded from the boy's side.

"Sara, put a repressor on that," he ordered.

The woman removed a small, oblong object and placed it near the wound. She pressed a button on the instrument and, instantly, the flow of blood stopped under the influence of a low-power force-field.

"Suction," McCoy said.

Sara pressed a flexible hose to the wound and the blood was drawn away.

"Now, I can see what I'm doing," McCoy murmured. "Sara, prepare an automatic IV, universal hemo factors, one liter," he ordered a moment later.

Snapping open a small kit, Ensign George removed a telescoping metal rod with a collapsible tripod base. Next, a plastic pouch containing a dark powder was hung at the top of the rod. She poured a liter of water from a storage jug into it. The powder dissolved almost instantly, and a red fluid began to run through a plastic tube into a needle which had been inserted in the boy's left arm.

"Good," McCoy said, his eyes glancing up briefly. "Now a type oh-oh scalpel."

Ensign George handed the instrument to McCoy and he pressed the tip of the slim cylinder against the boy's side. A short, bloodless incision appeared under the ragged hole around the spear shaft.

"Probe," he ordered.

Sara handed him a flexible, light-carrying tube with tiny waldoes on it, and he inserted it into the small incision below the wound. Plugging a lead from the other end into the medical tricorder, he studied the display on the instrument's tiny screen.

"Take a look, Jim."

"Ugly," Kirk said, looking at the black silhouette of the barbed spear point which had torn through the chest muscles and was buried in spongy gray lung tissue. "How are you going to get that thing out?"

"Watch. Minilaze, Sara," he ordered.

She handed him the tiny cutting tool. He made a clean incision through the tissue that had closed in around the barbs, the beam cauterizing as it cut. Then, grasping hold of the short, splintered stub, he gently pulled the head out.

"Sara, anabolic protoplaser, type zero."

He applied the tip of the instrument to the interior of the wound, slowly working it outward to repair torn veins and gashed arteries, and unite nerves and muscle fibers. Soon, all that was left was the closing of the jagged tear where the spear had gone in and the small incision below it.

"Type two protoplaser."

"Bones, wait," Kirk said, breaking his long silence. "I have the impression this is the boy's first battle; he only looks about fourteen or fifteen."

"So?" McCoy asked.

"How about giving him something to remember?"

"Like old Heidelberg, eh?"

"Something like that, Bones."

"If Starfleet finds out, they may lift my license,"

McCoy said, adjusting the protoplaser and setting to work.

When he finished, he looked at a puckered scar that made a semicircle on the boy's chest where the shaft had been. He made a quick scan with the medical tricorder and then switched it off.

"That'll give him some status with the other boys," he said. "And with a little rest, some hot soup, he'll be back on his feet in a day or two. Now the head wound."

He studied the torn flesh critically. "Good thing they shave their heads. Saves me the trouble of depilating him."

When he had finished, McCoy injected Alt with another dose of universal antibiotic and a stimulant to counteract the anesthesia. By the time the boy began to come around, the Federation medikit was safely back in its hidden compartment.

Alt's eyes flickered, then opened. "Who . . . ?"

"It's all right, son, you're going to be fine," McCoy said, giving him a gentle pat on the shoulder. "You're almost as good as new."

The boy's lips turned up in a hesitant smile.

"Here," Kirk said, handing the boy the broken spear, "a little souvenir." The boy studied the deadly object, turning it over in his hands and testing the razor-sharpness of the head with a finger. He looked down at his side and saw the lavish scar. His eyes widened.

"Truly, I am a warrior. But I thought only the Messiah could work such magic," he said, his voice touched by awe. "You have given me back my life. My father will be grateful."

"I hope so," Kirk said. "Not too long ago he was ready to cut our throats." He went to the rear of the van as Scotty and Chekov switched from off-key blues to equally off-key baroque. "Knock it off, out there," he called, opening the door a crack.

"My son, how is he?" It was the voice of Tram Bir.

"Fine, you can see him in a moment." Kirk turned to McCoy and hissed. "Get the boy's hood on. If his old man finds out that we've seen his face, we've had it."

The boy suddenly stiffened as he realized that, for the first time in his life, strangers had seen his uncovered face. His fingers touched his cheeks and then, in sudden panic, he grabbed the blood-soaked hood from McCoy's hand and jerked it down over his head. The slit that Kirk had made to get it off gaped open, exposing his features.

"My father will have you killed," he said. "You have seen my face. You hold my soul."

"Our only power is to heal," McCoy said. "Why do you think Beshwa go unhooded? Your magic is not ours."

"My father won't believe that. As soon as he sees me, he'll know you've seen my face."

There was a roar from outside and a banging on the door.

"When can I see my son?"

"Soon," McCoy answered, "very soon."

"I know a way," the boy said suddenly. "Who is the head of this family?"

"I guess I am," Kirk said.

"Then give me your hand. Don't question."

Kirk hesitated for a moment and then extended his right hand. Alt grabbed the broken spear which had almost ended his own life, gashed his own palm with the sharp point, and then did the same to Kirk. He took the captain's bleeding hand in his and gripped it tightly.

"Thy blood is my blood," he chanted. "Thy breath is my breath."

The door of the van jerked open and an impatient Tram Bir lumbered in. His cry of joy at seeing his son alive, sitting up, changed to a snarl of rage when he saw the split hood gaping open to reveal the boy's features. His hand dropped to his sword hilt.

The boy somehow pulled himself to his feet and staggered toward his father, holding his bleeding hand before him.

"We are of one blood, the Beshwa and I. We share

one tent." Strength exhausted by the ordeal he had been through, his knees buckled and he sagged at his father's feet. McCoy grabbed him before he fell, and laid him gently on the bunk.

"He'll be all right," he said, "but he needs rest and care." He beckoned to Tram Bir. "Look at our work and rejoice in your warrior son," he said, pointing to the scar. Tram bent over.

His hand left his sword hilt and he ran his fingers over the snaking ridge of flesh. He straightened, took Kirk's hand, and looked at the bleeding palm.

"The blood mingled," he muttered, "but Beshwa . . . ? This will need long thought. Care for the boy. I will decide what is to be done with you when we reach the place of our clan."

CHAPTER FOURTEEN

"Look on the bright side, Bones," Kirk said. "We're alive, we aren't tied up any longer, and we—at least I—have acquired a new family." He surveyed the thin pink line on his right palm and flapped the reins to get the neelots into motion. Slowly the caravan moved forward and took its place at the rear of the column. At the head rode Tram Bir and his warriors. After them came the carts of looted iron ingots. Following the carts came a morbid procession of neelots bearing the dead clansmen. Behind the caravan trotted a small rear guard. Ensign George rode in the van with Alt; Scott and Chekov were riding in the wagon.

After a short journey along the main trail, the column swung right and started up a narrow canyon that angled back into the hills. The land began to rise more and more steeply and the trail became rougher, twisting and turning back on itself as they rose higher into the hills. At last, as the caravan topped a small rise, Kirk saw their destination, a small valley surrounded by unscalable escarpments. The near end was protected by a high wall and a precipitous gorge with a strange-looking span over it.

A support structure of tall beams and bracing cross-pieces rose at the bridge's far end. From it, cables slanted down and attached to the other side. An advance rider had evidently brought news of the war party's approach, because the defensive wall which ran along the far end of the gorge was lined with women, children, and old men.

As the riders at the head of the column reached the bridge, they urged their neelots into a loose-jointed gallop and raced across, whooping as they went. The heavy, ingot-laden wagons were more cautious; they crossed one at a time, the flimsy span shivering and swaying under their weight as the cables stretched and twanged.

Scott, who had replaced McCoy at the brake an hour ago, shook his head in disbelief as the last of the carts made it across.

"That bridge couldna support sic a weight," he muttered. "Its design violates basic engineering principles. Why the load factor alone . . ." He lapsed into silence, making mental calculations to verify his conclusion that the structure had to collapse under the weight of the first iron-laden cart.

"As you so often point out, Scotty, theory's one thing and practice quite another," Kirk said. "Here we go." He eased the heavy caravan onto the bridge and started slowly across, the span creaking under their mass. Scott heaved a deep sigh of relief as they rolled off onto solid rock on the far side and drove through the narrow gate in the wall. Once inside, and driving among the randomly scattered, dome-like tents of the clan, the rear guard cantered past them.

A squealing groan arose from the other side of the gate, and Kirk rose and turned to see what was happening.

Two teams of neelots were harnessed to cables that rose over the wall to the high bridge support structure and then down to the far side. As their drovers urged them forward, the bridge slowly lifted until, now vertical, its far end towered above the wall.

"A perfect defense," Kirk said.

Sara, sitting on a bundle of trade goods directly behind Kirk, said, "But how could a nomadic people come up with such an elaborate structure?"

"Semi-nomadic," Kirk corrected. "They spend half of each year here. From the appearance of this place, they've evidently been doing it for hundreds of years. They've had time to work out the details. And they need something like that. When grazing is bad, the tribes start to raid each other."

As the body-laden neelots ahead came to a halt,

Kirk stopped the caravan. He sat watching as men and women went from animal to animal, pulling off hoods to identify the dead. There was no outcry, no demonstration. Mothers looked at faces of dead sons for a moment, turned, and walked silently away.

"Demonstrative bunch," McCoy said.

"At least they have a chance to see them one last time," Kirk replied. "Before, they were left to rot. I wonder what Tram Bir has in mind for us?"

As he spoke, the chief appeared from behind the van with two men bearing a litter. After his son was borne away to a nearby tent, he came up to Kirk, who had climbed down from the driver's seat.

"I've thought much about Alt's bonding," the chief said. "It is unthinkable that clan brotherhood should be extended to Beshwa, who bear no arms. On the other hand, it can't be denied that our blood has been mingled. If you are strangers, you must be killed; but if you are my kin, I can't order your death. The question has never arisen before. I shall present it to the Messiah when we reach him tomorrow, while you remain here."

Tram Bir's casual statement struck home like a dagger. Kirk kept his face impassive as he glanced at the sun. It was already getting toward late afternoon and there were less than two days left in which to reach Spock, get close enough with the nullifier to break the connection between him and Gara, and return him to sanity. The place where the Messiah was assembling the clans was a good day's journey away. Unless Tram Bir could be persuaded to take them with him, the *Enterprise* was doomed.

"In the meantime," the chief continued, "you can make yourself useful. The Messiah wants every clansman who can handle a spear and sword—even the elders."

As he spoke, a group of bandaged hillmen began to cluster around the caravan; some, who had been brought back on the captured carts, being borne on crude stretchers. Tram Bir gestured toward them.

"These are needed for the attack on Andros. With your powers, you must see that they are healed and ready to ride at first light."

McCoy surveyed the group dubiously. There were ten on stretchers and at least forty walking wounded.

"We are a small clan," Tram Bir added. "Without these, I will be forced to sit far in the rear during the gathering of the chiefs."

Of course, thought Kirk, sensing an opening; in a society like this, a leader's importance among his fellows is determined by the number of swords he can muster.

"Chief Tram Bir, come to the van," Kirk said suddenly. "There are weighty matters we must discuss . . . alone."

"Great as our skill is," Kirk said, "it may be that some of the more seriously wounded will need a few days' rest before they can join you. The others, however, can be ready to ride with you by dawn. But give thought to the future. When Andros is stormed, many of your men will fall. It is true that the Messiah's strength will grow when he converts those who survive in the city and they take arms in his cause, but your numbers will shrink. What about your place among the chiefs?"

He poured Tram Bir another cup of wine.

"The others will have their losses, too," the chief said. "Our ranking will remain the same."

"True," Kirk said, "but if your numbers shrank less than theirs, before too long you would be sitting in the front as a principal chief." Kirk paused to let his words sink in and then added, "Of course, if you send your wounded all the way back here to be healed, many will die on the way."

Tram Bir took another sip of wine and looked at Kirk thoughtfully for a moment. "So you wish to come with us. What's in it for you? If the Messiah decides you are strangers, you will only hasten your death."

"He won't," Kirk said. "From what you've told me

about what happened in Andros, it's obvious that he had spies from the city in mind when he gave that order about strangers. As for us, we are now of your blood; we wish to serve you as best we can."

"Neelot dung!" Tram Bir snapped. "We of the clans take such things seriously, but Beshwa are only interested in trade. You claim kinship to save your throats."

Kirk pursed his lips. "I know there would be good trading where the clans gather—excellent, in fact. There's no reason why in helping others one can't help oneself. How about a deal, Tram Bir? We'll come along to care for your wounded if you let us do a little business on the side."

Tram Bir pondered Kirk's proposal for a long, silent moment then nodded slowly. "So be it. There will be a feast tonight when Afterbliss has set. We will talk more of this then."

"Afterbliss?" Kirk asked. "The word is new to me. I have learned today that the clans have a new leader who converts all who hear his voice and that he gathers the clans for a holy war, but I have not been told what this thing is you speak of."

"You must have seen it," Tram Bir said, "a new star that moves swiftly through the heavens before dawn and after dusk. It is for this that we who have not heard the Messiah's voice obey his orders and march to join him with our dead."

"I know nothing of this," Kirk said. "We saw a strange new light in the sky two nights ago and again last night, but we didn't know what it was."

"We had word of its first coming," the chieftain replied. "Two days ago, a rider came from a western clan with word that the gods had sent a leader who was to remake Kyros into a holy place. As a sign of his greatness, they would place a shining city in the sky, a place where those who died for them would live forever. That night showed the truth of his words. We saw Afterbliss with our own eyes. No longer will the spirits of our dead sink into the ground and their bodies be left to rot! Tomorrow the bodies of those who died today will rise to be reunited with the souls that wait above.

"Yesterday another rider came with orders for us to raid the mining camp and destroy the bridge, so no more spearstone could be taken to Andros for weapons. After what we had seen, we obeyed without question. Tomorrow we hear the Messiah's words with our own ears!"

He rose. "Heal as many as you can. We ride as soon as there is light enough to see the trail tomorrow. Your woman will remain behind with my wives. I will give orders that she be treated well."

Before Kirk could respond, there was an angry bellowing from outside the van, followed by a Russian oath and a thudding sound. Kirk and Tram Bir dashed out and discovered the chief's oldest son, Greth, sprawled on his back clutching a dagger—and an angry Chekov standing over him.

Greth shook his head as if to clear it and got groggily to his feet, raising the dagger as he did so. He went into a half crouch and advanced slowly toward the Russian, whose fist was cocked, ready to deliver another blow.

"Greth! What's going on here?" Tram Bir barked.

"This *zreel* struck me!" Blood began to drip from under his hood.

"I had to," Chekov said. "This *cossack* pulled a knife on me."

"All right, Hikif," Kirk said, using the Russian's Beshwa name. "Why?"

"It's my fault," said Sara, who had been standing to one side. "Greth ordered me into his tent. When I refused, he grabbed me by the hair and tried to drag me with him. Hikif tried to stop him, and Greth started after him with a dagger."

"That was very wrong," Tram Bir said, his voice solemn.

Chekov nodded his head in indignant agreement. "I'll say it was. He could have killed me with that thing."

"You misunderstand, Beshwa," the chief said coldly. "You heard me give him Sahgor; you had no right to interfere. Greth may kill you if he wishes."

Greth snarled and jumped at Chekov, throwing him to the ground. His right arm rose to drive the knife into the young Russian, when Kirk sprang forward. He grabbed the hillman's wrist, and with a quick twist sent the weapon flying through the air. Greth scrabbled after it, but Kirk got there first and put a foot on the blade.

"Hold it!" he shouted. "You can't kill Hikif. He's your brother."

"That's absurd," Tram Bir said. "I have no Beshwa get."

"I didn't say you did," Kirk replied, still keeping his foot on the dagger, "but when your son Alt bound me to him with his blood, he bound himself through me to Hikif, who is my brother. So," he continued, "since Greth is Alt's brother and Hikif is mine, Hikif is Greth's brother's brother's brother."

Tram Bir stood for a moment, obviously bemused at his sudden accumulation of sons. "It sounds logical the way you put it, but I'm going to have to think about it for a while. Until I get it figured out, Greth, leave Hikif alone."

"But I want to kill him now," Greth said petulantly. He thought for a moment, and a foxy light appeared in his red eyes. "If one of my kin does me harm, clan law allows me the right to challenge. Isn't that so, father?"

"True," Tram Bir said, "but you cannot harm him if he doesn't accept." He turned to Kirk. "Your brother does well with his fists, but swords are another matter. He should know that my son has collected two-score heads in battle."

"I'm sure he has," Kirk said, looking apprehensively at the barrel-chested hillman. Dismayed at the sudden twisting of his inspired genealogy, he went to Chekov and whispered, "Easy does it. We can't afford a row."

Chekov nodded his understanding and made no re-

sponse when Greth planted himself in front of him
and said contemptuously, "Only Beshwa and women
are too cowardly to bear arms."

"Good bairn," Scott whispered to McCoy, when
Chekov accepted the insult impassively.

"But even a woman would respond to this!" Greth
leaned forward and spat in the Russian's face. A second later he went flying backward, as Chekov's fist
lashed up and slammed into his jaw.

Tram Bir gazed impassively at his prone son. "Your
brother's brother's brother seems to have accepted
your challenge," he said. He turned to Kirk. "My
condolences on what is to happen after the ceremony.
Greth is a fierce swordsman."

"Well, Mr. Chekov?" Kirk demanded coldly when
the hillmen had left.

"He was going to rape her," Chekov replied defensively.

"I wasn't talking about that," Kirk snapped.
"You're Beshwa, you idiot! You're never supposed to
have handled a sword in your entire life. If you don't
act as if you don't know one end of a sword from the
other when you get out there, you're going to blow
our cover. On the other hand, if you kill Greth, we
won't be in any better shape. Either way, we'll be
dead by morning. Well, we've got a couple of hours
yet. Maybe we can think of something. Bones, you'd
better get to work on the wounded."

It was almost dark when the clansmen came from
their multi-colored, dome-like tents and began to
gather in a circle at the far end of the valley. Minutes
passed as the sky blackened, and then a jubilant cry
rang out when the shining drop of light rose above the
jagged peaks of the mountains to the east.

"Afterbliss!"

As the new star mounted higher in the sky, moving
toward its zenith, a struggling, squealing neelot was
dragged forward.

Tram Bir, sacrificial dagger in hand, waited, his

lips moving in silent prayer. Then, as the tiny new
moon reached a point directly overhead, his knife
flashed up, glittering redly in the dancing light of the
torches held by the encircling throng. The neelot let
out one sharp, high squeal as the blade slashed across
its throat. It reared, spouting blood, and then fell
twitching to the ground.

Tram Bir held a bowl under the scarlet gush until
it was full and then raised it to the heavens.

"To Afterbliss!" he shouted, and brought it to his
mouth. "Thus shall we drink the blood of the Messiah's enemies!" He sipped the steaming blood and
passed the bowl to an elder who stood next to him.
The old man took it, repeated the cry, and touched it
to his lips in turn. Then he carried the vessel to the
waiting circle of warriors who passed it from mouth
to mouth.

There was a reverent hush as the shining pearl
dropped out of sight behind the western hills, and
then Tram Bir signaled for attention.

"Before the feasting there will be a test of swords.
My son Greth and the Beshwa Hikif will fight until
the gods decide on whose side honor lies."

An incredulous buzz rose from the crowd. *A
Beshwa?*

As his father retired to the sidelines, Greth pushed
his way into the ring. "Where is that cowardly
zreel?" he roared.

There was no answer for a moment, then Chekov
sidled timidly into the arena, awkwardly holding a
meter-long, broad-bladed sword straight out in front
of him. Greth, holding a similar weapon, advanced
slowly, hunching slightly forward. A titter of laughter
began among some of the young girls as Chekov just
stood there, staring at his sword as if he'd never seen
one before. Then, as his opponent came within striking distance, he raised it, holding onto the hilt with a
clumsy-looking over-and-under grip.

Greth gave a nasty laugh as Chekov backed fear-
fully away, his sword wobbling as if he couldn't control the shaking of his hands. The hillman made a

sudden lunge, bringing his sword down in a whistling slash intended to split Chekov from crown to crotch. The young Russian seemed doomed, but he twisted awkwardly away so the blow missed him completely. Cursing, Greth whipped his sword up again, hungry for the kill. Chekov stumbled backward and sideways, his clumsy, foolish-looking attempts at defense somehow deflecting every blow Greth tried to land.

Catcalls and jeers rose from the crowd.

"What are you waiting for, Greth?"

"Too old too soon?"

"Hey, Greth, having trouble getting it up these days?"

Stung by the taunts, the hillman rushed forward and unleashed a hammering attack that drove Chekov almost to the other side of the circle of spectators. Again, none of his blows landed; each time it seemed a thrust was sure to bite home, a clumsy, amateurish parry miraculously turned it aside.

Suddenly, his sandal heel caught on a protruding rock thrusting from the soil hard-packed by generations of clan feet, Chekov toppled backward.

Greth snarled and lunged in for the kill.

As Chekov's shoulders hit the ground, he threw up his blade in a desperate parry.

The down-coming stroke was deflected, but not enough.

Chekov screamed as blood gushed from a gaping wound in his stomach, jerked spasmodically, then lay still.

CHAPTER FIFTEEN

"How did I do?" Chekov asked, after he was carried into the van.

"Beautifully," McCoy said. "But you had me worried. You made it too realistic. Why did you stretch it out so long? You were supposed to go in there, let him get in a stomach cut, and take a dive."

"I wanted to make that cossack look like a monkey," Chekov replied and chortled. "Did you hear them hooting when I was being carried out?" He mimicked a mocking, feminine voice. " 'Hey, Greth, next time you take on a Beshwa, have your father hold him for you.' " The Russian looked down at the deep, bloody gash in his stomach and said soberly, "He almost had me at the end; I wasn't figuring on that fall. I may have been first sword at the Academy for two years straight; but if you hadn't thought of putting a duraplas body shield under all the rest, that cut would have sliced in fifteen centimeters and I'd be dead for real. Get that stuff off me, will you?"

McCoy nodded, and went to work.

"Where did all that come from?" Kirk asked.

"Mostly from the splint kit. The dermolastic on top looks like real skin," McCoy said as he peeled it off to reveal a ten-centimeter layer of solidified, foam-like material underneath. "That's used for making field casts. It's sprayed on and the foam sets in seconds." He pulled off the padding. Underneath that were the slashed remnants of two one-liter bags which still oozed a reasonable facsimile of Kyrosian blood.

"Our gore," McCoy said. "And lastly, a final precautionary measure in case Chekov's swordmanship wasn't quite as good as he thought—which it wasn't—" He snipped and lifted a thin sheet of dark material which was glued to Chekov's stomach. "That was tough enough to turn Greth's point. Instead of cutting in, it just skidded along the surface."

"From the splint kit again, I suppose," Kirk remarked.

"Right. It's a plastic that's sprayed over the foam to protect it. OK, Chekov, clean that red gunk off and then we'll call Tram Bir and show him another Beshwa miracle."

"How aboot the scar?" Scott asked.

"Oops, almost forgot that detail. Sara, what do you have in the way of makeup?"

"I don't know," she said. "I found a woman's bag among the other stuff we inherited, but I haven't had a chance to check through it yet." She went to the front of the van and, after a minute's searching, came back with a small bone box containing a thick red substance and a brush.

"That should do the trick," McCoy said, and drew a fine pink line diagonally across Chekov's stomach. He eyed it critically. "You know," he said, "that's one of the neatest jobs I've ever done."

A rapping came from the rear of the van. Kirk opened the door and saw Tram Bir standing in the darkness.

"I've come to apologize for my son," he said. "The killing was not done well. It was bad enough to challenge a Beshwa, but to bungle the job and make a fool of himself in front of the entire clan . . . gah! I've half a mind to leave him with the women tomorrow."

"Don't be too hard on him; as you may have heard, the Beshwa have strange powers," Kirk said and turned. "Hikif, come here."

As the young Russian bounced jauntily out of the caravan, Tram Bir let out an incredulous gasp.

"I . . . I don't believe it!" he said. "Greth must have sliced you to the backbone."

"He did," Kirk said easily. "Without our sister we couldn't have saved him. She called on Azrath and his power came down and filled her. When she touched Hikif, his gut closed before our eyes. Look!"

Chekov stepped into the light that came from the open door of the van and pulled up his vest. Tram's eyes widened when he saw the thin pink line.

"This is why our sister must come with us when we go to join the Messiah with you," Kirk said.

"No," Tram said flatly. "Women must stay behind when the warriors ride. If I let her come along, my men would demand a new chief." He clapped Kirk on the shoulder. "But bring your brothers and come to the feasting. I want to hear what Greth says when he sees the dead walk in." He turned to go.

Kirk thought quickly. Without Ensign George, their chances of getting close enough to use the nullifier on Spock were nil.

"Wait," he called. "What if your warriors wanted our sister to come?"

"There's no chance of that," the chieftain replied.

"Perhaps not," Kirk said, "but let her speak to them in her own way after the feasting."

It was still dark when there was a banging on the van door.

"First light is almost here," a hill voice called. "We leave with it."

Kirk sat up with a groan and clutched his throbbing head with both hands. There was a stir as the others pulled themselves out from under their fur coverlets. Except for Sara, the others didn't seem to be in any better shape than their captain.

"I'll go out and hitch up the neelots," Sara said brightly. "I don't think any of you are up to it."

"Who brought me home, Bones?" Kirk asked as she exited briskly into the gray of early dawn.

"Beats me," McCoy said. "The last thing I remember was Chekov doing a Beshwa version of the kazatski, while Scotty was speculating on whether a neelot stomach would do for a proper haggis. You know, Jim, I never could understand the Scots predilection for making puddings from chopped-up sheep's lungs."

Kirk made a face, but Scott didn't respond. He was too busy nursing a hangover.

"Oh, well," Kirk said, "I suppose this, too, will pass." He got to his feet, poured water from a jug into a basin, and splashed his face. The van door opened and Sara came in.

"All ready to roll," she said. "If you're driving, Captain, you'd better get up there. Tram Bir's ready to leave."

"Glad you're coming with us, Ensign," Kirk said. "After that dance of yours, if Tram Bir had said no, his men would have strung him up right there and elected you chief."

"My dop is a woman of many talents," Sara said demurely.

"Don't be so modest, Ensign. You did provide the body, you know."

Kirk went outside and climbed into the driver's seat. Tram Bir waved him into position behind the provision carts. As he pulled up behind them, there was a snarl of clan horns. Then, Tram Bir and his warriors at the head, the column moved out through the gate and across the drawbridge.

Two hours later, they were back on the east-west migration trail.

"Tell me, Jim," McCoy said, "what do you think our chances are of getting within striking distance of Spock?"

Kirk shrugged. "Not too good. If you were in his shoes, what would you expect us to do?"

"Probably something pretty much like we're doing."

"Right. What I'm hoping is that he'll expect us to come in disguised as hillmen. There's another thing in our favor, too. He doesn't know about the radiation storm and how desperate our situation has become up there. As a result, he may not anticipate a try as crazy as this one—at least not this soon." He glanced up at the sun and made a quick mental calculation. "I know this vehicle sticks out like a sore thumb but, with luck, it may take a few hours for word about strangers in the camp to get to him. According to the map, it's going to be about dusk when we get there, and some big ceremony involving the dead we're bringing is planned. That should keep him busy for a while. What's more, Tram Bir is on our side."

"How?" McCoy demanded.

"Before we got too drunk last night, I suggested to him that he ought to hold off on asking the Messiah about us until he was in a position to ask a favor— like maybe after the first battle. I think he'll go along with that because we're a fairly valuable property, and he'd like to have us around as long as possible. Besides, I think he has designs on our little ensign."

McCoy chuckled. "I wouldn't doubt it. When she tossed her G-string to the crowd on her final exit, I had a few myself."

There was a long silence during which Kirk thought of what lay ahead. Finally, he said somberly, "Every time I think of the odds we're facing, I wonder if I shouldn't have given Chekov's suggestion more serious consideration."

"You mean using a shuttlecraft and phasers?"

"Yes. My veto was based on the dynamics of Earth history. Maybe they don't work the same way here."

"Could be, Jim," McCoy said, "but it's too late to do anything about it now. You ordered Sulu to refrain from any direct action until he heard from you and," he added wryly, "I don't think even your voice is loud enough to carry a hundred and fifty kilometers."

Kyr's red bulk was dropping toward the horizon as the clan column emerged from the widening valley onto the northern limits of the great coastal plain, a gently rolling land covered with short, feathery fronds of reddish Kyrosian grass. The setting sun's rays tinged them a deep maroon, making it look as if the land had been painted with blood.

Kirk gestured toward the south. "Andros is someplace down there."

McCoy nodded and pointed off to the right as something caught his eye. "Look," he said, "company . . ."

In the distance, another clan column was moving on a converging course. As minutes passed and the two groups came closer together, white-sheeted dead could be seen heaped on long, flat-bedded carts.

"Looks like they had a raiding assignment, too," McCoy said.

As they rode on, more groups of riders came into view, most of them from a westerly direction. Then they topped a slight rise, and the great gathering came into view. Tent clusters, each marking the camping place of a clan, formed a rough horseshoe, the open end facing south. Each grouping was separated from the one on either side by an open space of at least a hundred meters distance. It looked as if, in spite of their new-found unity, a certain amount of hostility and mutual suspicion remained. Smoke began to rise into the still air as cooking fires were lighted. In front of each tent stood spears, one for each occupant, their burnished heads gleaming in the last rays of the setting sun like fire-dipped pinpoints, a flickering, changing scatter of earthbound stars.

Dominating the curved upper part of the horseshoe was a great black pavilion, a long, low rectangle that stood in marked contrast to the dome-shaped tents of the clan clusters. Directly in front of it, a tall pole had been erected and from it hung a black banner. Caught by a momentary gust of wind, it rippled out, displaying a large white circle in its center, the symbol of Afterbliss. Surrounding the pavilion, one every three meters or so, stood armed hillmen, weapons at the ready.

McCoy jerked his thumb at them. "It looks like visitors just don't wander in unannounced."

Kirk nodded in somber agreement. "Nobody ever said that getting to him was going to be easy. Spock may be crazy, but he's shrewd."

A hundred meters or so behind the pavilion, a black tent stood by itself. Behind it was a semicircle of domed shelters that were larger and more elaborately decorated than those in the clan area. An ornate banner flapped in front of each.

"Looks like he wants his chiefs close at hand," Kirk said.

A speaker's platform had been erected in front of the pavilion. Before it, at a distance of two hundred meters or so, white-wrapped bodies had been placed in concentric circles, heads facing inward. More were being placed in position as additional contingents of hillmen arrived with their dead.

"Looks like they're going to cremate them," McCoy said, as clansmen began to carry in armfuls of wood from a huge pile to one side. They continued to watch as they drove closer.

"Uh, uh," Kirk said. "They've got something else in mind. Look where they're putting it." Four long arms of wood were growing from the circle of bodies to form a cross, each arm pointing to a different point of the compass. Hillmen scurried back and forth like ants, adding wood until each pile was at least fifty meters long and a meter and a half high.

As more bodies were carried in, Kirk made a mental calculation and then whistled. "Spock really bloodied his troops," he said softly. "There must have been a clan raid on every settlement on the perimeter." His brow furrowed. "Why would he waste men like that when he needs them for his attack on Andros? Once he has the capital, the outlying villages will stop resisting."

McCoy shrugged. "The Messiah moves in mysterious ways."

As the clan column neared the encampment, a rider trotted out and spoke briefly to Tram Bir, who was riding at the front. He nodded and sent Greth, who rode next to him, off with the message. Then he angled the column to the left, skirting the eastern edge of the horseshoe until they reached an open space at the end. Kirk pulled the caravan to a halt on the inner side of the assigned space. Around them, clansmen began unloading baggage carts with practiced haste, and umbrella-like tents were soon springing up. The carts bearing the clan dead were driven into the open center area, and stiff bodies, stinking after two days in the hot sun, were carried off and laid shoulder to shoulder with the rest.

Chekov and Scott, who had been riding in the van, got out and began to stroll among the clansmen. They hadn't got more than twenty meters before Tram Bir, who was supervising the placement of the tents, stopped them and said something, jerking his thumb toward the caravan.

"What's up, Scotty?" Kirk asked as the two came up.

"It looks like we're under house arrest. The birkie says that i' we go wanderin' aboot barefaced, we might end up wi' oot our heads."

"So tell him we'll wear hoods."

"I did. He says we canna. Relatives or nae, we're still Beshwa."

Clan pennants began to ripple as night breezes blew in from the sea. The sharp scent of burning wood filled the air, and Tram Bir's men began preparing their evening meal. Then, as leather provision sacks were opened, the stench of *vris* wafted across the campsite.

McCoy sniffed. "You know, I think I'm finally getting used to that smell," he remarked.

"No wonder," Kirk said with a grin, "you ate enough of it at the feasting last night."

"I . . . *what?*" McCoy exclaimed, his face incredulous.

"At least three helpings. Isn't that right, Mr. Scott?"

"Och, aye, Captain," Scotty said. "A' the least. Wolfed it down like it was his last meal, he did. I remember thinking then that there was nae accounting for taste."

"There certainly isn't, *haggis eater,*" retorted McCoy, not knowing whether to believe what he'd been told or not. He sniffed again, gagged slightly, and disappeared behind the van.

As Kyr set, a mournful howl of clan horns began from the direction of the Messiah's black pavilion. Hillmen began to move from clan tents out into the grassy area between the arms of the horseshoe-shaped encampment.

Kirk moved forward, too, forgetting Tram Bir's admonition, but was turned back by a guard. He thought for a moment, and then clambered onto the van's top for a better view. McCoy and the rest climbed up after him.

Hillmen bearing torches stationed themselves along each of the long arms of piled wood extending from the circle of corpses. They stood silently, waiting. There was another hooting of horns and the flaps covering the entrance to the Messiah's tent were thrown back. Marching out of the pavilion came the clan chiefs in order of precedence, Tram Bir nearly last. Moving in single file, they circled around the platform that had been erected and formed a line in front of it, facing the dead.

There was silence until the Messiah appeared, then a great roar went up. He walked slowly forward to the platform and mounted its steps. He stood for a moment, head bowed. Clansmen, as if on cue, scurried out from the sidelines with large leather sacks. Liquid gushed as they drenched the kindling.

The Messiah raised his head and cried in a ringing voice, "Give fire to the gods!"

The waiting hillmen flung their torches onto the oil-soaked wood. It ignited with an explosive *whoosh,* and a cross of flames leapt into being.

Lit by the leaping flames, the Messiah began to speak. In spite of himself, Kirk felt a shivering tingle run up his spine as the hypnotic voice rolled out over the assembly.

"The gods have touched me and ordained that I work their will through you, their instruments of holy wrath. Tonight we have kindled a flame which shall spread out against the darkness until all Kyros shines with holy light.

"I am the hammer of the gods, and I will forge

your souls in battle until all dross is driven forth and
they, like shining blades, arise at last to their reward
in Afterbliss."

His left arm stabbed toward the east. The thousands turned as one and watched the glittering point
of light climb over the horizon.

"There, the souls of those who died for me already
walk the golden streets. But disembodied souls can
never know the joys of battle, wine, and surging loins.
And so all men have always feared that final sojourn
in the joyless halls of death. But now, for you who
follow me, who serve as swords to win a world-wide
holy state where I may rule as viceroy of the gods,
they have prepared a golden place. There, warrior
bodies unite with warrior souls and find each day of
their reunited, eternal life a new delight. Behold! The
first to fall depart."

An awed moan came from the watchers as a shimmering pink opalescence sprang into being around the
white-swathed bodies. Then, as a low, throbbing
sound began, the dead seemed to stir.

"They live again! The gods summon them to Afterbliss!"

As if in response to the Messiah's words, the dead
clansmen began to rise into the air, slowly drifting
upward accompanied by the awed moaning of the
warriors. Faster they rose, and faster, like snowflakes
falling upward, they vanished into the darkening sky.

"A tractor beam from the *Enterprise*," Scott whispered.

Kirk paced silently for a moment and then faced
the others.

"After that demonstration, there'll be no stopping
Spock once he begins to march. His men will turn
into berserkers when the fighting starts. Now . . . they
know that death in the field is a passport to a warrior's
idea of heaven."

"And they move against Andros tomorrow," Mc-
Coy said somberly. "Once through the gates—what
we saw in that village yesterday is just a taste of
what's going to come. What do we do now?"

"We use the only weapon we have—Sara. She's the only one with half a chance of getting close enough to Spock to do any good. We know she turns him on—that episode at the inn the morning they beamed down shows what kind of animal he's turned into. Look, Bones, he's bound to have some kind of celebration for the clan chiefs tonight. We've got to get Sara in there to dance. The way she had Tram Bir's men howling shows that, once she's turned her dop loose, she can be as hypnotic as Spock."

"And what if the nullifier doesn't work?"

"Then we'll kill him," Kirk said flatly, "I don't know how, but we'll kill him."

The two stood silently and watched as subdued hillmen streamed back to their clan areas. Then a familiar voice caught their attention and Kirk peered down into the darkness. Tram Bir had just returned and was questioning one of the guards.

"Where's Greth? He was supposed to be here an hour ago."

The guards shrugged. "I haven't seen him since he rode off just as we entered camp."

"The Messiah wants an exact accounting of our clan at once," Tram Bir said in an irritated voice, "—men, weapons, and neelots. I don't have time to prepare it; I have to dress for the Messiah's feasting. Have Greth attend to the counting as soon as he arrives." Muttering to himself, he was turning to go when Kirk jumped down and called to him.

"Was the Messiah pleased with your gift of spearstone?"

"I couldn't get close enough to tell him about it," Tram Bir grumbled. "Obeisance was by ranking of clans, and I was so far back in the line that the ceremony started before I could get to him. It's thanks to your healing that my numbers are enough so I wasn't the last of the chiefs. As it is, though, I'll have to sit in the last row as we feast." His unhappiness about his placement was evident in his voice.

"Preference shouldn't depend on numbers alone," Kirk commiserated. "If there were just some way you could attract the attention of the Messiah . . . I know that if you just had a chance to talk with him he would see at once—as I did—that you are a leader among leaders, a warrior whose fierce courage and wisdom in battle fit him to be chief of chiefs . . ."

"I agree," Tram Bir said, waving a hand to interrupt Kirk. "But how could I attract the attention of one so mighty?"

"We Beshwa are practical men," Kirk said. "If you stood at the Messiah's right hand, we couldn't help but benefit. I think I know a way."

"What is it?" Tram Bir said eagerly.

"A gift only you can offer. God-touched though it is, the Messiah's spirit inhabits a man's body, even as yours and mine. Think back to last night—what happened when our sister danced?"

CHAPTER SIXTEEN

Kirk shivered and pulled his cloak tighter about him as he paced near the Beshwa caravan. Cold gusts of wind blew from the west, bringing smoke and fine ashes from the still-smoldering embers of the fires. Thunder clouds building on the western horizon held a threat of rain. To the north, the sky began to lighten with the first flickerings of an aurora. Two of Kyros' moons had set and the third wouldn't rise for several hours. The camp was quiet except for occasional shouts and bursts of raucous laughter from the Messiah's pavilion.

"What's taking him so long?" McCoy muttered.

"I told him to wait until the Messiah had several cups under his belt. Chag Gara was as much a lush as he was a lecher. When Spock was imprinted, the process wasn't selective." Kirk glanced at the sky. Stars were winking out as the thunderclouds rolled eastward.

"I wonder what's going on up there?" McCoy asked.

"It's getting ready to storm, what else?"

"No, I mean on the *Enterprise*."

"They're sweating us out—and getting ready for evacuation, just in case. Radiation will reach redline in fifteen hours or so."

"Where will they go? . . . If they have to, that is," Chekov asked.

"I told Sulu to break the crew up into groups of forty to fifty and to scatter them among the neighboring city-states. Four hundred and twenty-five strangers showing up in one place would be a bit too much. After the life they've had, it isn't going to be easy to be exiles on a backward mud-ball like this;

but they're all bright people, they'll survive. At least they won't starve. Thanks to Scotty's money machine, they'll all be coming down with full purses."

"And when the Messiah comes?" Chekov asked.

"They'll fight."

"Stop it, you two," McCoy said. "You're having a wake before the patient is dead."

Sara came out of the van. "The costumes are ready," she said. "Come on in and try yours on. Wait till you see what Scotty made for me."

Scott looked up from an improvised workbench as they came in. "How do you like this?" he said, holding up a stylized golden mask of a creature half cat and half woman. "We had to figure out some way to cover Sara's face so Spock wouldn't recognize her."

"Beautiful," McCoy said, picking it up and turning it over in his hands. "But how did you make it?"

"I used gold foil from the trade goods and the rest from your medikit. Sara modeled the features from that foam for making casts. I used that as a matrix for the gold foil. When the foil was shaped, I removed it and sprayed the inside with duraplast to give it strength. A little trimming, a couple of eye holes, and that was that. Not a bad job, if I do say so myself."

"What about the rest of us?" Kirk asked. "Spock isn't exactly unfamiliar with our faces."

"Ready to wear," Scott replied, pointing to some grotesque masks on the bunk beside him.

Chekov's voice called from outside. "Captain, somebody's coming from the direction of the Messiah's tent. It looks like Tram Bir."

It was.

"Hurry," he said as he came out of the darkness. "You're to entertain the Messiah. When I described what he might expect, he became most interested." Anxiously, he added, "She will do as well as she did last night, won't she?"

"Better," Kirk promised.

It took them only a few minutes to get ready. The men wore flowing cloaks made of a patchwork of

multicolored furs with collars of bristling orange
feathers. Kirk's mask was a neelot's head; Chekov's,
an exaggerated clan-style hood with a pointed top
from which sprouted more orange feathers. McCoy
and Scott wore the heads of antlered, deer-like animals.

Kirk slung a Beshwa drum over one shoulder as
McCoy and Chekov took up their thirty-seven
stringed instruments. Scott experimented with a Kyrosian horn that curved from the mouthpiece down to
his waist, where it swelled into an ovoid.

"Reminds me of my bagpipe back aboard the *Enterprise,*" Scott murmured sadly.

"I'm glad our dops know how to play these crazy
things," McCoy said as his fingers ran a masterly
arpeggio on the strings.

Ensign George came down the van steps to join
them. Her face was adorned in the delicately styled
golden mask. It disguised her completely, but was as
deliciously female as the face it covered. Her body
was wrapped in a long black cape.

Kirk called to the impatient Tram Bir, "We await
the Messiah's pleasure."

Tram nodded and gestured for them to follow.
They moved away from the Beshwa caravan under
a cold glitter of stars, and marched toward the loom-
ing black of the Messiah's tent.

Driving gusts of wind raced through the area whip-
ping the Messiah's banner and buffeting the sides of
the huge, ebony pavilion. Tram Bir exchanged a
few words with the soldiers who guarded the entrance.
The flaps were flung back, and the party passed into
a small antechamber.

Inside, guards gathered around them curiously.
Tram Bir said something that Kirk couldn't quite
catch to a soldier who seemed to be in charge. He
glanced back at the group, then nodded; and Tram
moved through a heavy curtain which separated the
antechamber from the main body of the tent.

From beyond the curtain, Kirk heard the growl of

a mass of voices, sporadic laughter and shouts. There
was the clatter of crockery and an occasional crash as
a drinking bowl was dropped. Kirk was given a brief
glimpse of the interior as the curtain parted again. He
got an impression of depth, darkness interspersed with
the light of hot-burning torches, and many clan chieftains. Tram came back out.

"The Messiah awaits your performance," he said.
"But it is his order that you be searched carefully before entering."

Kirk glanced at the others in his party, then made a
sign of acquiescence. He took a step, brushing closer
to Ensign George.

"Almost home, Ensign. Turn on the nullifier," he
whispered.

Without a sign that she had heard, Kirk saw her
left hand move to cover a thick wristband, one of
several on her right arm. She gripped it tightly, acti-
vating the mechanism.

Tram disappeared behind the curtain again and the
guards moved toward them.

"Open your clothes," one guard growled. "Messiah
orders that you be searched—completely." His smile
displayed decaying, crooked teeth.

"For what?" Chekov began.

"Hikif! You know better than to question the Messiah's command," Kirk snapped. One of the guards
moved to Chekov, while two more pinned his arms.
The search was brief, painful, and thorough.

When several of the guards turned to Sara, she
stepped back. Kirk opened his mouth to order her to
cooperate, then closed it quickly.

She pirouetted away from the men and giggled. In
a low voice, she purred to the guards. She turned her
back to the *Enterprise* party and parted her cloak.
The guards gasped.

One nudged another whose mouth was partway
open. "She couldn't hide much in that outfit," he
said and grinned appreciatively.

The others nodded in agreement. Sara giggled again

and demurely closed her cloak. She rejoined her fellow officers.

"That was quite a performance," Kirk whispered.

"Captain, I haven't even *begun* to perform. Just wait!" she said.

The chief guard barked an order and his men snapped to attention and marched to the curtain and parted it.

Kirk caught Sara's hand. "Do your best," he whispered. "There's a lot at stake."

"Aye, Captain," she whispered. "Trust my dop." Her hips moved sensuously and she gave a provocative little bump before moving ahead of the four men.

Kirk nodded to his officers and led the party through the tent doorway.

Directly ahead was an oval of hard-packed earth. Ranged around it were intricately woven mats and husky chieftains lounging on throws of lush fur. Large trays loaded with wine jugs and exotically colored and strangely shaped fruits and nuts were at their elbows. Serving men scurried in and out of another entrance directly across from Captain Kirk and his fellow officers. The lift of a hand or a bellow from the first rows of men sent a servant scuttling to his side to replenish his wine jugs and fruit bowls. Further back, the men were less lavishly dressed. They sat on bare neelot hides, and their signals to the servants were not answered with such alacrity. Kirk suspected Tram Bir had been in their ranks, on the very perimeter of their ranks, before he had gotten the Messiah's ear and told him of Sara's charm. Now he sat importantly in the very first row.

The Messiah was at the head of the oblong tent. He lounged on a raised dais draped with a silken, vermilion fur, the exact shade of the slashes of color beneath the eye holes of his ink-black, hooded mask. Guards were ranked in a semicircle behind him. Oil lamps on long poles flickered and smoked and sent eerie, grotesque shadows up the sides of the tent.

Kirk gave a roll on his drum to announce their

presence. When he dropped his arms, the guard led the Beshwa party forward to the edge of the circle of hard-packed earth.

The Messiah waved a long-fingered hand. "Welcome."

The performers bowed and Kirk murmured, "Peace and long life, Messiah."

"Live long and prosper—Hirga of the Beshwa," the Messiah responded after a pause.

Tram Bir stood, swaying slightly, and raised a nearly empty wine bowl. "Bring more torches that we may have more light to see the performance!" he shouted.

Instantly, serving men scurried in bearing torches. They drove the sharpened pole ends into the ground around the edge of the tamped earth circle.

The Messiah moved his hand in an impatient gesture. "We're waiting, Beshwa. Entertain us."

Kirk bowed and moved his band to one side. Scott, Chekov, and McCoy squatted and began to tune their instruments. Kirk set his drum on the ground and went to Sara, who still stood at the edge of the circle with her golden-masked head lowered, her slender body completely hidden in the long cape. As she lifted her hands to the clasp at her throat, his eyes caught the thick band on her wrist and he breathed a silent prayer. Then he took hold of the cape and whirled it away. There was a momentary silence as the tent full of men leaned forward to ogle the shapely body of the young ensign.

Kirk took his place behind the drum, glanced at his friends, and relaxed his mind, allowing the talent of his Beshwa dop to flood through him. As his fingers lightly caressed the drum's taut membrane, bringing a soft murmur from it, McCoy and Chekov drew bows across their instruments, evoking steadily rising, pulsing notes. Scotty joined in just as the sound seemed on the verge of passing from the audible range. Kirk's palms came down on the drums, interweaving a beat into the cascading sounds.

Sara's arms uncurled to reveal jutting breasts that

were barely covered by golden circlets of the same
material as her mask. Below, she wore a small golden
triangle. A sparkling jewel nestled in the dimple of
her navel. A transparent, shimmering fabric, light as
air, floated from her shoulders and, rather than hid-
ing her nudity, enhanced it. Her hips made sensu-
ous movements in rhythm with the music, and her
gold-tipped fingers and toes punctuated the beat.

Beshwa it wasn't, but the sighs and groans of the
watching hill chieftains told Kirk that no one would
object. Ensign George was pure, unadulterated, wanton sex. She pirouetted slowly, and the jewel in her
navel danced to the music that spiraled from the
Beshwa instruments. Although she moved teasingly
among the clansmen seated nearest the circle, her
graceful and nimble feet danced her out of their
reach as they lifted hands toward her shapely body.
Her smooth shoulders swayed, making the filmy fabric
that enveloped her a shimmering cloud of color
through which her creamy body glowed. The torchlight flashed and glittered from her mask.

Gracefully she whirled, coming ever closer to the
Messiah. He sat impassively, but his eyes followed her
every movement. Her arms wove graceful patterns as
her body undulated before him.

Not close enough, Captain Kirk said to himself, as
he gauged the distance from her arms to the lounging
man. The range of the nullifier was only one meter.
He increased the tempo.

As Kirk's drum boomed faster, Chekov and Mc-
Coy followed along with a frantic sawing of their
bows across their instruments. Scott hit and held a
single high, pure note. Ensign George twirled across
the hard-packed floor, her body a frenzy of orgiastic
movement. She came to a halt before the Messiah with
her arms raised beseechingly. Only her round little
belly with its glittering jewel continued to dance. Her
slender, swelling hips began to punctuate the beat and
she slowly inched her feet forward. She was dancing
solely for the leader, now.

Slowly, gracefully, she lowered her arms from above

her head and reached out and ran her hands over his neck and shoulders. Then she sank to the floor at his feet.

Clan chiefs burst into wild applause. "More!" they screamed. "More!"

The Messiah held up his hand for silence and then motioned to Kirk and the others to rise. They stood, bowing from the hips.

"Beautifully done," the Messiah said. "You will find that I am not ungenerous. Observe."

He made a sudden, commanding gesture. Guards pounced. There was a fierce, futile struggle. Their masks were torn from their heads; then the four men were dragged forward.

"Holy one, how have we displeased you?" Kirk said humbly.

"Displeased, Captain Kirk? To the contrary, I'm delighted. I have fond memories of my last encounter with Ensign George. It was most kind of you to bring me such a lovely gift. Bind her!" he snapped to the guards, his voice suddenly ugly. "Take her to my tent!" He watched as Sara's wrists were lashed together and she was dragged from the pavilion. Then he beckoned to Tram Bir to step forward. The chief sidled forward and stood before the Messiah like a small boy expecting punishment.

"It was at your suggestion that I allowed these 'Beshwa' to enter my presence, was it not?"

"I thought they would please you, Messiah."

"What was my directive concerning strangers?"

"To kill them, Messiah. But these saved the life of my son. He joined them to us in blood. Also, they are great healers. The force I brought here is stronger because of them."

"So your son Greth told me earlier, especially of the dead man who was walking around whole an hour later." He shifted from Kyrosian to English. "Your healing was too ostentatious, Dr. McCoy. Coming as a Beshwa was a most ingenious disguise, but to come equipped with a medikit? As soon as Greth told me of yesterday's events, especially those involving Ensign Chekov, for whom he seems to have a pronounced dislike, the identity of the party was obvious."

He reverted to hill dialect and spoke to the murmuring, confused hill chiefs. "This one," he said, pointing to a cringing Tram Bir, "betrayed me. As is the custom, his oldest son will succeed him as chief. He and the demons who came in Beshwa guise will be given as a burnt offering to the gods before the rising of Kyr. Remove them!"

CHAPTER SEVENTEEN

As the Messiah watched, five long, sturdy poles, butt ends set deep in the ground, were readied in the center of the circle once occupied by the clan dead. Then Tram Bir and the four *Enterprise* officers were stripped and lashed securely to the poles with leather thongs. A cutting wind brought the first stinging drops of cold rain.

"Don't you wish you'd stayed aboard the *Enterprise,* Captain?" the Messiah said. "Your bridge is a much cozier place. But you'll be warmer, come morning. There's enough wood and oil left to take the chill from your bones when we greet Afterbliss just before dawn. I think a burnt offering to the gods of a chief who disobeyed my orders, and spies who sought my life, will have a salutary effect on my followers. I'll see you in a few hours." He turned to go.

"Hold it," Kirk snapped in an authoritative voice.

"Yes, Captain?"

"Killing us is pointless. Something has happened you don't know about."

"Yes?"

"Your clans may take Andros for you, but when you march against new cities, you are going to have to have other miraculous raisings of the dead to convince them you are what you say you are and sweep them up in your crusade."

"A logical assumption, Captain. That's why the gods have provided me with Afterbliss."

Kirk studied the black-robed figure for a moment. So cool, so logical, and yet so crazy. There had to be a way of getting under that paranoid overlay to the original, clear-thinking mind. Emotional appeals were useless since, Kirk thought, they would drive the Messiah further into paranoia. But cold logic might yet somehow get through to the original mind and stir it to revolt against the madness that enchained it. With a tremendous effort, he forced himself to appear as cold and dispassionate as if he were discussing an intriguing new concept in theoretical astrophysics.

"Your mistake is in believing the *Enterprise* will continue to follow your orders," he said quietly.

"Indeed? I've been careful to make only reasonable requests of Mr. Sulu. He complies because he thinks he's buying the time necessary for you to recover the warp-drive modulators. I certainly wouldn't be stupid enough to give him an order he'd have to refuse— such as using phasers against Andros." He tapped the tricorder he was wearing under his robes. "As long as I have this, it is illogical to think the *Enterprise* will be uncooperative."

"You can't expect help from an abandoned, radio-active hulk," Kirk replied. "And that's what the *Enterprise* will be by this time tomorrow. Since you disabled our warp-drive and beamed down here eight days ago, something catastrophic has happened." As precisely as if he were feeding data into a computer, Kirk described the rapidly peaking radiation storm and its inevitable effects on the helpless starship.

"Indeed," the Messiah said when Kirk finished. "What you've told me correlates directly with the change in weather patterns and the auroral displays of the past several nights. As soon as I finish my mission down here, I'm looking forward to calculating the origin of the storm from the data in the ship's computer. The sub-space manifestation is most intriguing. In fact," he added, "once my campaign gathers enough momentum so that it no longer needs my personal supervision, I'm thinking of moving permanently to the *Enterprise*. I have no one to play chess with down here. What's more," he said with a sudden change in voice and manner, "Ensign George doesn't have exclusive rights. I'm looking forward to brightening the nights of Nurse Chapel and a few of the others."

Kirk's control wavered. "Damn it, Spock!" he burst out, "can't you understand that—"

"I am not Spock, I am the Messiah," the other interrupted coldly.

"I don't care what you call yourself," Kirk replied hotly. "Can't you get it through your thick head that the crew will have to abandon the *Enterprise* in less than twelve hours? You may have extraordinary powers of persuasion, but your voice alone can't conquer a planet for you. There will be a group from the *Enterprise* in every city you attack; and General Order One or no General Order One, they'll use every scrap of the knowledge they'll bring with them against you! You may have a brilliant mind, but it doesn't stand a chance against four hundred and twenty-five of the Federation's best. You can kill us, you can conquer Andros, but after that, your movement is doomed to certain defeat. Nobody denies that the gods have touched you and that you have great work ahead, but it obviously isn't to be done here. Otherwise they wouldn't have sent the radiation storm. Call the *Enterprise*—they have the coordinates of this spot —and have them beam all six of us up. The gods must have some other world in mind. Once our warp drive is operational again, we'll take you there."

The Messiah peered at Kirk through the night. The third moon had risen, and gleamed fitfully through the clouds that scudded overhead. The wind gusted higher, bringing with it bursts of cold, sleet-like rain.

"Perhaps the one who was known as Spock would have been convinced by your reasoning," the black-robed figure said, "but his mind knew only a universe limited by cold, mechanical equations. I have been touched by powers beyond. When physical law and divine law conflict, there can be only one outcome. Since Afterbliss is important to my plans, the gods will not permit it to be destroyed. It would be illogical. And now if you'll excuse me, gentlemen, Ensign George is waiting." The Messiah turned and strode away into the night.

McCoy let out a long sigh. "Good try, Jim," he said,

"but the input from Chag Gara has Spock's mind so twisted that there's no way you can make a dent in that crazy logic. A paranoid *knows* his beliefs are an accurate reflection of what really is."

"I know," Kirk said, "but I had to make the try. Are everybody's hands tied as tightly as mine? If just one of us could get loose—"

"I don't know about the rest of you," McCoy said, "but I might as well be in a straightjacket."

There was a long silence between the captives. The wind gusted around them. After a time, Chekov said somberly, "Poor Sara . . ."

"Poor Sara, my foot," Scott grumbled. "She'll still be alive come sunup, and that's more than I can say for the rest of us. If we don't freeze to death long before then," he added, shaking with cold as another blast of frigid wind brought more drizzling rain. The guards who had been left behind cursed the downpour, turned their backs to the biting wind, and pulled their cloaks up over their heads.

"I wouldn't bank too heavily on Sara's lasting the night," McCoy said. "Spock may kill her before morning."

"Why?" Kirk asked.

"I've a hunch he's not going to get the reception he's expecting. Sara's changed a lot in the last week, but she's a far cry from the bitch in heat that Spock coupled with at the inn. Her dop's no longer in control."

"She might play along with him to save her own hide," Scott said. "Anything's better than burning."

"Sara wouldn't do that," McCoy said. "Unless . . ." His voice trailed off.

"Unless what?" Kirk demanded.

"Unless the filter stage on her implant still isn't working properly. When she was dancing, she seemed to really enjoy turning everybody on."

"If that she-cat she's linked to is still dominant," Kirk said thoughtfully. "Maybe she's been playing a game during the whole trip."

"And maybe we're both getting as paranoid as

Spock," McCoy said. "If we keep it up, pretty soon we'll be suspecting each other. Look, Jim, she tried to get to him with the nullifier. It's not her fault the damn thing didn't work. I can't say I'm surprised it didn't though," he added gloomily. "Nothing's been working right ever since we hit this planet. First the implants go haywire. Then we hit Spock with a dart that's supposed to knock him out for a couple of hours, and he's back on his feet in a matter of minutes. Then we take off on a crazy expedition whose only purpose is to get an electronic widget close enough to Spock's implant to put it out of commission. And when we do—against odds so astronomical I don't feel like trying to calculate them—nothing happens! But damn it, it should have. All the Vulcan variables were taken into account in its design."

"There's one thing you haven't considered," Kirk said.

"What's that?"

"What if she turned the nullifier off before she started to dance?"

"Why should she?"

"If her dop is in control, she may have decided that being the mistress of the master of Kyros offers a way of life quite a bit superior to that led by an ensign on a starship."

"I don't know," McCoy said, "I'm not sure of why anybody does what he does any longer."

An irate mumbling came from Tram Bir, who was trussed to the post farthest from Kirk and McCoy.

"What's he saying?" Kirk asked Chekov, who was bound to the stake nearest the hillman. "The wind is taking his words away."

"He wants to know what the crazy gabble is that you're talking. He says he never heard anything like it."

"You wouldn't believe it if I did tell you, chief," Kirk called, switching to Tram Bir's own tongue. Then he added, "I know an apology isn't going to mean much, but we didn't intend for things to end up this way."

Tram Bir shouted something, but again the wind whipped his words away.

"What now?" Kirk asked.

"He says that he hopes they light your fires first so he has the pleasure of watching you burn."

"You know, Jim," McCoy said, "somehow I think we've lost a friend."

The guards shivering in front of the black tent snapped to attention as they recognized the torch-bearing figure nearing them.

"It is as you ordered, Messiah."

"Good. Go to your chief and tell him I said you are to have hot wine. I have no need for you; the gods guard me."

The guards touched their hands to their hoods and hurried off into the chill darkness, cloaks flapping behind them in the gusting wind. The black-robed figure threw open the flap of the tent and stepped inside. A girl, trussed and nearly naked, lay on a raised pallet covered with soft furs. A tiny flame burned in a heavy stone lamp resting on a low table to one side. On a rug on the other side, barely discernable in the dim, flickering light, a blanket-draped figure lay, curled tightly in a foetal position, knees drawn against chest and forehead pressed against knees.

The girl looked up through sultry, half-closed eyes and smiled. A knife flashed and cut the cords that bound her feet and hands. A bending, a puff of breath, and the lamp flame died. There was a faint rustle in the darkness as a robe fell to the floor.

The rain had finally stopped, but the five tied to the stakes were so miserable and numb with cold that they hardly noticed the change. As the hours crawled by, the wind died and the sky began to clear. Stars appeared and then, as the tiny second moon rose, there was enough faint light for Kirk to make out the silhouettes of guards who stood like statues, leaning on their spears. There was a sound of something moving in the darkness, and then a barked challenge, as a long, dark shape appeared out of the night.

"You guard well," said a familiar voice.

"Messiah!" Hands went to hoods in salute as a figure climbed down from the driver's seat of the Beshwa caravan.

"Minds are being twisted," he said in a strange, distant voice. "Sub-chiefs slip from tent to tent, whispering. These Beshwa demons send mind tendrils out to snare my clans, just as they did with this traitor here."

A muffled appeal came from Tram Bir, but was roughly cut off as a guard clubbed him.

The figure motioned one of the guards to approach him, and there was a quiet exchange. Then the hillman led some of his fellows off into the darkness. Moments later they returned, some with arms full of wood, and others carrying oil sacks. The van door was opened and the burdens placed inside. More wood was brought and more oil, until the vehicle was full. Then the thick fabric cover of the cargo wagon that made up the front half of the caravan was thrown back part way, and the men were cut down, bound again, gagged, and dumped inside. When Tram Bir was dragged forward, his masked head hanging, the black-robed figure raised a hand.

"Not him. Take him to his tent. I have other plans."

As Kirk and the rest lay helpless on the hard floor of the wagon, the cover was drawn forward and they were left in total darkness. The wagon rocked slightly as someone climbed into the driver's seat.

"Wait, Messiah. We will get our neelots."

"For what?"

"We'll ride as guard."

There was a contemptuous laugh. "Against what? Who would dare to harm the Messiah?"

"These did."

"These *tried,* but demons in Beshwa bodies are not impervious to fire. They must burn now before they touch more minds. Thank you for your concern, but

I must be alone when I make an offering of their enemies to the gods."

The caravan moved off. After a while it stopped. Somebody climbed up to join the driver, and there was a brief exchange of whispers. The caravan began to move again at a slow walk. Minutes passed.

Then suddenly, from behind, came the sound of shouts, first faint, and then louder as more and more voices seemed to join in. There was the cracking of a whip, and the wagon began to jounce violently as the neelots burst into a gallop.

There were grunts of pain as the bound men were slammed from side to side, unable to brace themselves as wagon wheels slammed into rocks and bounced high into the air. Suddenly, the caravan jolted to a stop.

"Slash the oil bags. We'll do it now," said an urgent voice.

From the back of the van came the sound of the doors being opened. At the same time, a sound of hammering and prying came from underneath the wagon at the point where it was joined to the van.

"Now!"

A moment later, there was an explosive *whoosh* and then the fierce crackle of burning wood.

"Beautiful!"

Kirk twisted, startled at the sound of Sara's voice.

The crackling grew to a roar, and thick smoke began to seep under the canvas-like covering. A whip cracked again and the wagon moved forward. There was a sudden, slamming jolt, and then it picked up speed. Choking, Kirk squirmed into a sitting position and pushed up with his shoulders until he was able to force the heavy covering back and get his head over the wagon's edge.

He blinked, eyes watering, momentarily blinded by the sudden glare. Jouncing along behind them at the end of a long wooden boom came the van, spouting flame high into the air like a blast furnace, and lighting up the plains like a giant searchlight.

The shouting from behind grew louder, and then screaming clansmen came pounding out of the darkness, lashing their neelots to even greater efforts as they emerged into the fiery light.

A black-robed figure was out in front, spear couched low.

He shouted a command, waving first to the left, then to the right. The riders split, spreading out on either side in an encircling movement. The leader veered in as he passed the front of the wagon. His arm went back and his spear hurtled forward. The lead neelot screamed, reared, and crashed to the ground, dragging the others down with it. The wagon jackknifed and ponderously overturned.

The last thing Kirk saw was the van rushing toward him like a flaming juggernaut.

CHAPTER EIGHTEEN

A faint touch of gray appeared in the eastern sky as the clans assembled before the torch-ringed platform in front of the black pavilion and waited silently for the command that would send them flooding down upon Andros. There was a snarl of hill horns.

A black-robed, black-and-red-hooded figure appeared, walked slowly to the platform, and climbed the stairs heavily.

A roar went up from the thousands assembled and they pounded their spear butts in unison on the hard-packed earth.

"Messiah! Messiah!"

He stood staring out into the pre-dawn darkness for a moment, as if oblivious to the frenzy of his followers, and then, with an obvious effort, raised one hand jerkily in a plea for silence. His voice was strained, and cracked as he spoke.

"With the rising of our heavenly home, we ride against the godless. The gods send Afterbliss at my command. Behold!"

The clans pivoted as one when he turned to the east and threw out his arms.

The magic moment came—and passed.

A growing uneasiness began to run through the crowd as no glowing sign rose above the distant mountaintops. Minutes dragged by, and the eastern sky grew lighter as high, floating clouds turned molten red in the first rays of the rising sun.

A querulous muttering began, first hushed and then louder and more demanding. The figure on the platform dropped his arms at last and tried to speak. His faltering words were drowned in shouted questions as warriors broke ranks and began to press closer.

173

On the platform, a sudden sparkle of shimmering light made them freeze in place. A tall, white-robed apparition with slanted eyebrows and pointed, alien ears appeared next to the Messiah.

The Messiah backed up a step, throwing up his arms as if to protect himself. His wail of distress and loss was cut off as a hand shot out and gripped him where his shoulder met his neck. He slumped to the platform, a puppet without strings.

The white-clad figure faced the stunned, silent crowd and began to speak in a powerful, resonant voice.

"Do not fear. The gods have not sent me to bring you harm. And they have only pity for this poor, mad creature here whom demons used to work their will. Do not wait again for Afterbliss; there never was a golden city for the dead. You were tricked by an empty ball of light set burning in the sky by demons' spells."

"But our dead? We saw them rise!" a clansman cried, his voice shaking.

"But not to a new life. Once a spirit sinks into the ground, it cannot return. The demons took the dead you brought and hid them in the clouds, so you would believe their false messiah's lies. Behold."

Heads craned upward as he pointed into the sky. High up, like distant birds, white specks began to descend, circling, floating lower and lower until, as gently as snowflakes, rigid, white-swathed bodies came to rest in the circle from where they had been lifted the night before.

"Return to your old ways. If you change them, let it be because you, yourselves, have decided that they should be, not because some evil magician has dazzled your eyes. Will you obey?"

All heads bowed in assent.

"See that you do. The gods have one more command. The chief Tram Bir has been ill used. Restore him to his place. Henceforth he shall sit first among the chiefs."

Again heads bowed.

"I go," the figure said and then added a warning. *"If you again heed evil voices calling you to war, I may return."* The voice softened. *"And now, disperse. Go back to your hills and be at peace among your-selves and with the people of the plains."*

The figure raised his right hand, thumb extended and middle and fourth fingers spread in a vee.

"Live long and prosper."

Then, the hum muted by the open air, the flick-ering carrier wave of an Enterprise transporter sur-rounded the two men and they slowly, slowly disap-peared.

CHAPTER NINETEEN

"Where is Mr. Spock?"

Kirk smiled at McCoy's question. "He said he saw no reason for wasting time on postmortems. When I left the bridge, he had every computer bank tied into the science console and was punching up a storm. If it were anybody else, I'd say he was ducking this meeting because of embarrassment."

"I wouldn't rule that out entirely, sir," Ensign George said with a sly grin. "When I passed him in the corridor, he gave me an awfully cool nod."

Kirk looked down at a yellow pad on which he had jotted some notes. "Let's get to work," he said. "We'll be in contact with Starfleet Command before too long, and I've been trying to pull together a preliminary report. I think I have everything down, but I wanted to check with all of you to be sure I haven't left out anything important."

"I'm afraid Uhura and I can't be of much help, sir," Sulu said. "There was so much to do between the time we beamed you up from the burning wagon and the time we sent Mr. Spock down to get the Messiah —along with lowering the bodies from their orbit —that nobody had the time to fill us in on what's been going on down there. About all I've been able to figure out is that the Messiah was Chag Gara all the time, and that for the last ten days Mr. Spock has been in a catatonic state."

"You're right with two exceptions," Kirk said. "One when Spock, controlled by Gara, stole the crystals; and the second explains why our kidnapping attempt in Andros failed. The paralysis drug worked, but it was Chag Gara that was paralyzed. He had no control over his own body, so he brought Spock out of suspended animation and sent him through the trap door on the roof of that closed cart, to put McCoy and I out of operation so he—Gara—could escape."

"But was Mr. Spock unconscious all that time?" Uhura asked.

"Except for those two times, yes," Kirk replied. "Spock explained it to me on the bridge. The melded minds could only control one body at a time. When Spock was linked to Gara, two things happened simultaneously. First, the emotional input was so strong that it overwhelmed the filter stage of the implant and established a two-way link so that Chag Gara had immediate access to Spock's mind. Secondly, the emotional impact from his dop caused Spock such intense psychic pain that his will went into a state of shock. He was aware of what was happening, but there was nothing he could do about it; he was a marionette with Gara pulling the strings."

"No wonder he acted so strangely when he beamed up the first day," Uhura said. "It must have taken Chag Gara a while to get used to controlling somebody else's body."

Kirk nodded. "The instant the link was established, Gara found himself hooked into a fantastic organic computer. With his new-found intelligence and the ability to use it logically, he immediately saw how he could use the *Enterprise* to further his crazy plans."

"So that's how he recognized Ensign George in the plaza," Sulu said. "Since Mr. Spock was Gara's dop rather than vice versa, he had complete access to his memory."

"Right," Kirk said. "Obviously, he realized immediately that if we found out where he lived, we'd head there, which was the last thing he wanted since that's where he kept Spock. Losing him would have meant losing his new-found power, so he made a beeline home, wrapped our unconscious first officer in a blanket, and hauled him off to a safe place. I imagine he had a bad moment when the neighbors tried to stop him, but knowing precisely how to give the neck-pinch got him out of that one."

"There's still one mystery left," Uhura said. "How did Sara realize that the messiah wasn't Commander Spock?"

"His ears," Ensign George said. "Chag Gara had one thing planned, but I had another. Mine was to grab the communicator and the tricorder, sneak out of camp, and then call the *Enterprise* and hide until a rescue party was sent down."

"And what was the messiah supposed to be doing all that time?" Sulu asked.

"Nothing. I was going to sell him the idea that a willing partner was more fun than an unwilling one so he'd untie me. Then, when he had other things on his mind, I was going to bop him on the head with the lamp beside the bed. But before I could knock him out, I had to get that hood off; that hardened leather cap it goes with makes a darn good helmet."

"What about the hill taboo against exposing the face?" Uhura asked.

"He evidently thought that what he had in mind was more fun in the dark, and blew the lamp out. While I was taking off the hood, my fingers encountered some singularly unpointed ears. 'If this ain't Spock, then that must be Spock,' sez I to myself, thinking about the figure on the floor. So I waited until Chag was completely preoccupied with what he was doing, and then let him have it on the back of the head. Then I hoped over and slapped the nullifier bracelet on Spock's wrist. Once the link was broken, he snapped out of his catatonia and took over immediately. Since the locator circuit on the communicator was out, he came up with the idea of setting the van on fire so the *Enterprise* could get an infra-red fix and determine our beam-up coordinates—just as it did when Chag Gara lit that flaming cross to indicate the location of the bodies to be beamed up."

Ensign George made a wry face. "We intended to get far enough from the camp so the blaze wouldn't be seen, but I mustn't have hit Gara hard enough. We were barely out when he and his men were swarming after us like hornets. I thought we'd had it when Gara speared that neelot and we went over, but—"

She was interrupted by a call from the bridge.

"We're ready to warp, Captain, the crystals are installed."

"Good, I'll be right up. Mr. Sulu . . ."

"Warp Six, if you please, Mr. Sulu," Kirk said as he settled down in his command chair.

"Aye, aye, sir," Sulu replied crisply, and punched in the command.

"Mr. Spock—" Kirk turned toward the science officer.

"Have you ever thought of going on the stage?"

"No, sir. Why?"

"Your performance last night was superb: all the emotional nuances were just right. You played the role of Chag Gara so convincingly that I had no reason not to continue to believe you were Spock."

"But I was, Captain," Spock said blandly.

"I mean Messiah Spock."

"But I wasn't. Chag Gara was the Messiah."

"I know that now," Kirk said defensively. "All I was trying to say was . . . Oh, to hell with it. I'm glad you're back and everything finally got ironed out, though I'll admit that I got confused when the messiah on horseback—or neelot-back as the case may be—rode up alongside the messiah driving the caravan."

The turbo-lift doors hissed open and McCoy stepped out. Kirk broke off his conversation with his first officer with a distinct feeling of relief.

"That was a little too close for comfort, Jim," he said.

Kirk nodded. "But we beat radiation redline by several hours. Once we're out of the storm area we'll contact Starfleet and feed them our data. Maybe they can figure out where it's coming from."

"That won't be necessary, Captain. The answer is quite obvious."

Kirk turned and looked at his science officer. "Is it, Mr. Spock? Would you enlighten us, please?"

"I believe that is my usual function," Spock said, cocking an eyebrow. "The storm is coming from Epsilon Ionis, a black-hole binary."

"We considered that, but it's impossible. That double is thirty light years away. If the companion star has novaed since we checked it out last month, it will still be three decades before radiation from the explosion could reach Kyros. Nothing can go faster than the speed of light."

"That's interesting, Captain," Spock said. "I was under the impression that we were exceeding that by two hundred and sixteen times at this very moment."

"I was talking about normal space, Mr. Spock. Subspace is quite a different matter."

"Indeed it is," the Vulcan replied, "and the storm is coming through it from Ionis at Warp Ten."

"But how?"

"We have a fascinating situation here, sir," Spock explained. "With Ionis we have a black hole going around a recent nova in a highly elliptical orbit. During the last several weeks it's been rushing toward perihelion, scooping up more and more radiation as it accelerates in. Since the gravitational field of a black hole is so intense that radiation cannot escape, internal pressure built up to the point where the space-time continuum itself warped and the energy pouring in from the nova primary is spouting into sub-space like water from a giant fire hose. It is an unfortunate coincidence that the other side of the warp is in the area around Kyr. It's really quite simple, Captain—if, of course, you stop to think about it."

"Thank you, Mr. Spock," Kirk said. "I'm happy to see that your recent messianic activities haven't impaired your analytical ability. One more question: how long before that black hole will be far enough along from perihelion so that its energy output will no longer be a problem?"

"Not more than two weeks, sir," Spock replied.

"Good. We'll return to Kyros then and complete

our survey." He turned to McCoy and said in a voice loud enough to be heard by Spock, "I understand that Mr. Spock has withdrawn from the survey team. Pity. For a while there he seemed almost human."

Not giving the first officer a chance to reply, Kirk went on, "By the time we get back, Bones, you should have all of Gara's paranoid kinks straightened out. We'll block all memory of what happened up here. When he goes back to preaching, he'll be able to use that power of his to heal wounds instead of making them." He stretched luxuriously. "You know, Bones, I think before we leave Kyros for good, you and I have a bit of shore leave coming after our hair grows back." Kirk brushed his fingers along the Beshwa cut he still had.

"Sounds good," McCoy said. "I'd like to see how Ker Kaseme is getting along."

"That isn't quite what I had in mind," Kirk said.

"It surely isn't *vris*—is it? I've had enough of that—"

Kirk replied loudly in a vigorous negative, cutting the doctor off.

"But why else would you want to visit? Sara's dop couldn't have anything to do with it, could it?"

"Why, Bones, you know me better than that."

McCoy grinned. "Do I, Jim?" He turned to go and then paused. "Shall I drop by your quarters a little later? We still have some unfinished business—namely, an almost full bottle of Canopian brandy."

Kirk nodded. It was going to be a good evening —an hour or so with an old friend, and then to bed, to march once again through the mountains of Persia with Xenophon and his beleaguered hoplites.

"Would you care to join us, Mr. Spock?"

The Vulcan looked up from the science console, lifted an eyebrow, and said, "If you'll excuse me, Captain, I already have my evening scheduled. My inside look at the depths of emotion has merely added another datum to my conviction that the Vulcan way of programming leisure time is much more logical."

"Three-dimensional chess, Mr. Spock?"

"Of course, Captain."

"With Ensign George, perhaps, Mr. Spock?"

"With the ship's computer, sir. I prefer an opponent who can keep its mind on the game."

ABOUT THE AUTHORS

THEODORE R. COGSWELL is an established science fiction writer, with many books and stories to his credit. He was the secretary of the Science Fiction Writers of America and he now writes for their magazine, *Forum*.

CHARLES SPANO, JR. is a new writer who has become a devoted Star Trek follower and an authority on all the characters, events and background of the series.

THE EXCITING REALM OF STAR TREK

☐	24193	**PERRY'S PLANET** J. C. Haldeman III	$2.95
☐	24636	**STAR TREK: NEW VOYAGES** Marshak & Culbreath	$2.95
☐	24174	**WORLD WITHOUT END** Joe Haldeman	$2.95
☐	23756	**STAR TREK: THE NEW VOYAGES 2** Marshak & Culbreath	$2.95
☐	24634	**SPOCK MUST DIE** Jim Blish	$2.95
☐	24637	**DEATH'S ANGEL** Kathleen Sky	$2.95
☐	24633	**VULCAN** Kathleen Sky	$2.95
☐	24638	**FATE OF PHOENIX** Marshak & Culbreath	$2.95
☐	24635	**PRICE OF PHOENIX** Marshak & Culbreath	$2.95
☐	24674	**SPOCK THE MESSIAH** T. Cogswell & C. Spano, Jr.	$2.95

Prices and availability subject to change without notice.

Buy them at your local bookstore or use this handy coupon for ordering: